M000167161

PRIVILEGED

CARRIE AARONS

Copyright © 2017 by Carrie Aarons

All rights reserved.

No part of this book may be reproduced in any form or by any electronic or mechanical means, including information storage and retrieval systems, without written permission from the author, except for the use of brief quotations in a book review.

This is a work of fiction. Names, characters, businesses, places, events and incidents are either the products of the author's imagination or used in a fictitious manner. Any resemblance to actual persons, living or dead, or actual events is purely coincidental.

Editing done by Proofing Style.

Cover designed by Okay Creations.

Do you want your **FREE** Carrie Aarons eBook?

All you have to do is **sign up for my newsletter**, and you'll immediately receive your free book!

This one is for you, little girl. May you chase all of your dreams.

CONTENTS

Chapter 1   1
Chapter 2   7
Chapter 3   11
Chapter 4   15
Chapter 5   21
Chapter 6   27
Chapter 7   35
Chapter 8   41
Chapter 9   47
Chapter 10   55
Chapter 11   63
Chapter 12   67
Chapter 13   73
Chapter 14   81
Chapter 15   85
Chapter 16   93
Chapter 17   99
Chapter 18   107
Chapter 19   113
Chapter 20   119
Chapter 21   125
Chapter 22   135
Chapter 23   143
Chapter 24   149
Chapter 25   155
Chapter 26   163
Chapter 27   169
Chapter 28   175
Chapter 29   179
Chapter 30   183
Chapter 31   189
Chapter 32   193

Chapter 33	197
Chapter 34	201
Chapter 35	207
Chapter 36	211
Epilogue	215
Do you want a free book?	221
Also by Carrie Aarons	223
About the Author	225

1

NORA

The black Mary-Jane's strapped to my feet, too expensive to even hold a candle to the things I used to call shoes, clack along the floors of the hall in timid steps. I wobble, not used to heels and even more unfamiliar with the two-hundred-year-old oak panels beneath me. Tapestries that pre-date my birth, my mother's birth, and probably her mother's birth adorn the walls, casting an elegant and old-worldly feel to the building.

Mint, cigar smoke and some kind of expensive after-shave scent have to be permanently embedded in the walls, because no matter where I've walked in this school, I can never escape the smell.

And the stares. *Oh*, how they stare.

As if it wasn't bad enough being the new girl on the first day of senior year of high school, my luck dumped me here. In the middle of the richest, most entitled, most elite bunch of people I would probably ever breath the same air as. And these were only their teenagers.

I pull on my uniform, the green and white plaid skirt suddenly feeling way too short, even though I know it's well past my knees. Judging by the girls lining their lockers, looking me up and down, I'm the most modest one of them.

"Is that the American?" I hear a whisper from my right and try to deflect it, try not to flinch.

Because on top of being the new kid, the outcast ... my life has been displayed in living color on every magazine rack in the city of London for months. These kids have already made up their minds about me, and it's not even five minutes into the first day of school. They've seen the pictures of me in a bikini, hanging out at the local pool in our hometown of Pennsylvania. They've read the headlines about my gold-digging mother, and our obnoxious American ways. Every childhood memory, every interview from a random stranger back home, even the snippet they got from our supposed neighbor and friend ... it's all been paraded around for the gossip satisfaction of this country's best and brightest.

I know that Mom and Bennett told me to lift my head high, to walk on water. To act like I'm even in the same stratosphere as these people. But ... this is high school. Even back home, it was vicious for me. And I'd grown up there, in the same dirt and poverty that everyone else had.

Winston Preparatory Academy? This was a whole different ball game. With its years of history, remembrance walls of students who'd gone on to be world leaders and CEOs, sixty thousand dollar a year price tag and etiquette rules I would never be able to remember.

My white-collared shirt and blazer stick to me by the time I make it to my locker, and there are so many eyes boring holes into my back that I'm sure the blush has moved from my face all the way down to my toes. Pulling the introduction folder the severely monotone school receptionist had given me when I'd first been dropped off from my new leather satchel, I flipped to the section with my locker number.

Except, these weren't like normal, metal and combination lock lockers. They were wood, each with a tiny school crest carved into the bottom left corner. The locks were a numeric keypad, like an upgraded ATM machine. And I was even more intimidated than I'd been nervously walking the unfamiliar corridors to get here.

Keying the code in, the light on the keypad flashed red at me. I tried again, but to no avail. Maybe they'd given me the wrong combination? Jeez, I was probably the only girl in this school who had basic high school problems. I read the short paragraph about how to reset the lock, and made quick work of it. Sighing as the lock finally flashed green, I was ready to open the door and hide my flaming face in the darkness of the locker.

Red and white balloons popped out as I swung the wood door open, and paparazzi pictures of my mother and her new husband lined the walls like wrapping paper. Somewhere inside, Miley Cyrus' "Party in the USA" began to play, loud enough for the entire hallway to hear the twangy chords.

Humiliation, bright and red like an angry sore, tore down my spine, making my body flush hot and cold. Of course I didn't know anyone here, so I couldn't know who did this. Only that they'd gotten into my locker before I could, and they were sending a message.

A group of girls standing across the hall, their skirts rolled, makeup flawless, with dress-code violations to the ceiling, burst into laughter. I turned, my mouth probably hanging open at the prank. One of the girls raised a sassy eyebrow at me and then they all fell into line as she walked away, while the rest of the students in the hall pointed or laughed.

Realizing that Miley was still singing, I slammed the locker shut, drawing even more attention to myself.

"Stop looking like a lamb panicking before slaughter and they might leave you alone."

A voice invades my embarrassment, licking at the side of my neck with its deep timber and British undertones.

My head turns without my brain telling it to, my synapses firing of their own accord. The first thing that meets my eye is the Winston crest embroidered on a standard-issue school blazer. And then they travel up, higher and higher until my neck is almost tilted all the way back.

The first student who has bothered to address me is tall ... standing more than a foot taller than my figure. Dark green eyes, almost as dark as the blazer his broad shoulders fill out, meet mine. In them are judgment, a hint of anger, and a whole lot of sarcasm. His words, spoken from lips the color of crushed cherries, don't fit his expression. This raven-haired boy, more like man, isn't giving me advice.

He's issuing a warning.

The sheer shock of his presence, and the wealth and superiority he exudes, almost knocks me over. He's waiting, his jaw ticking with amusement at my gaping silence.

When I can't seem to find words, and the tunnel vision that locks only to his face keeps getting worse, he reaches out. Big, dexterous fingers pick up a lock of my fiery red hair off my blazer.

He twirls it in his fingers, regarding me as my eyes follow the movement with child-like awe.

He leans in, the clear scent of the woods after a thunderstorm hitting my senses. "Or don't. I'll have fun watching them have their way with you. You don't belong here, *peasant*."

His insult, spoken like the dirtiest curse word he could muster, snaps me out of my reverie. I snap backwards, my hair falling back onto my shoulder as his grin, cold and malicious, mocks me.

I should say something, defend myself, fight ... but I've never been a fighter. I've never wanted the attention. To be honest, I've never known what I wanted.

So I turn on my heel and bolt.

What these elites didn't realize was that I had no intention of becoming one of them. I was happy to play the outsider, to not belong. The only thing I could wish for now was to get through the next year as painlessly and unseen as possible. They could have their status, their high society, their rules. I wanted none of it, and at least I knew that.

It wasn't my fault I'd been thrust into this life, and I wanted out as soon as I could get it.

A whir of red rounds the corner at the end of the hall, and the precisely controlled disdain that had been fueling my veins burns and rolls again.

I'd call our first meeting a success.

Nora Randolph, I would never refer to her as a McAlister, must be eliminated. Everything she is, everyone she is now connected to, is dirty. And now that I have her as a pawn, we can finally expose her dear old stepdad for what he is.

A murderer.

The bell for period one sounds, a perfect chiming melody that I know Nora must not be familiar with. Back in whatever hole of a town she crawled out of, they probably bang on a cowbell or something equally as barbarian.

My classmates mill about, the younger ones scurrying with books loaded in their arms, running for their first classes.

Me? I just lean against the row of lockers that Nora's resides in, metaphorically sharpening my claws like a tiger's. Not that senior year needed to be here for me to reign over Winston Prep, but I could almost smell the fresh blood in the air.

This school taught and raised the most elite of the elite.

Parliament members, world business leaders, royals, athletes ... they all sent their children here. To the famed academy that created them, to the school that rewarded with connections and a certain air on a résumé.

And I was at the center of it all. Asher William Frederick of the Cornwall Frederick's. My father was one of the most powerful men in the British government, as all of my family members were influential on the London society scene.

"Are you already bending women to your will? At least give the rest of us a day's head start, mate."

I don't have to turn to know that Edward Le Deux just slapped my shoulder, his voice scratchy from the rough night we had a mere eight hours ago. Ed, my best mate since we were nine, had decided it would be a great idea to throw a massive party in his father's grand library as a way to commemorate summer term ending. It was a miracle either of us were standing here, bright eyed at 7:30 a.m.

"Nope, that one I just intend to shock and frighten." A sneer curls my lip.

"Whatever you say, mate. You have such odd relationships with these birds. If I didn't know better, I'd say you're one of those whips and chains blokes."

"Sod off." Like I was going to talk about how I liked to fuck.

"Love you too, chap. Anyways, let's get going. Professor Hugh is only going to make so many exceptions for us this year."

I didn't care about that. My early acceptance at Oxford was secured. I barely needed to float through the year and grease each teacher with my Frederick charm.

"Or we could go to The Gentleman's Lounge and work off the exhaustion of last night." I raise an eyebrow. A lap dance sounds like just what the doctor ordered.

Ed groans. "You tosser, I'd love nothing more. But my mother will beat me mad."

My best mate was typically all mouth and no trousers, and this instance was no different.

"Fine. I'll go to class only because it's the first day."

But I took one last look at the end of the hall before I followed Ed.

I expected the arousal from exuding power over someone else. It was in my breeding to strike fear with a well-placed smirk, or exert control with just a movement of my fingers.

What I didn't expect was the tightness in my balls from the sight of her. The papers didn't do her justice; she might be American but she was a pretty little thing. All long legs and impoverished innocence. She doesn't know what this world is like, what people like the ones I associate with could do to her.

What I could, and intended, to do to her.

As I took my seat in Eighteenth Century European History, my head still swam with the piss of anger, and the plans of destruction that were yet to come.

3

NORA

W hen I think of home, I think of Pennsylvania. The small town where I grew up is a simple town, full of simple people. There are three stoplights, one elementary school, a diner and a man-made lake that the town considers a community swimming pool.

I was born there, I was raised there, and I thought I would live out the rest of my life there. My mother was the manager at The Honey Time Diner, we lived in a quaint two-bedroom ranch, I went to school, and at night we'd sit on the deck drinking lemonade or hot chocolate, depending on the season.

It was she and I against the world, our little bubble of two was all I'd ever known.

And then Bennett Charles McAlister, or as the world knew him, the Duke of Westminster, rolled into our lives. The third in line to the British throne, the notorious royal's town car broke down on the road outside of our house in early May of this year. He'd walked the half a mile up our driveway, mud and dust caking his shiny black shoes and impeccable suit.

The minute he'd entered our home, and the second he and my mother had breathed the same air, I knew that the bubble had burst. It was no longer just the two of us, that much was clear from the minute their eyes had connected. I'd felt like I was witnessing a star explode, or God perform a miracle ... the moment two people fell in love was rarely seen by others yet I'd watched it blossom and unfold right there in my living room.

In all eighteen years I'd been alive, I'd never seen my mom look at a man the way she'd looked at Bennett. It was apparent from the get go that this was the man she'd been waiting for, the literal prince coming to save her from her average life. And luckily, he didn't mind that his common princess had a daughter.

So here we are, living in London. If it weren't happening to me, and if it hadn't been such a nightmare thus far, I would think the past three months were straight out of the *Twilight Zone*. My mother meeting Bennett was one thing. But to be wearing possibly the next King of England's ring on her finger, to be marrying into the royal family? Sometimes I had to pinch myself when I woke up in the residence of Kensington Palace that we now occupied.

But with the good came the bad. And while my mother had found her happiness ... members of Parliament, the press and even those closest to her husband-to-be were crucifying her. Calling her a gold digger, questioning her motives, digging up any piece of insignificant dirt on her and running it for the masses to see.

And apparently, that crucifixion extended to me.

I'd expected to walk into Winston today and go virtually unnoticed. I was no one, I had no money, I wasn't upper crust like the rest of these kids. I was simply a tourist, staying for a temporary amount of time until I vanished out of their lives. I hadn't expected the stares, the curses, the whispers.

And I certainly hadn't expected the teenage James Bond who'd hypnotized me and basically told me to go to hell. His commanding presence still sat in my bones, that perfect English bone structure with the devious green eyes and mysterious dark hair were tattooed on the back of my retinas.

The way he'd touched me, no ... not even touched me. He'd simply held a lock of my hair between his fingers, yet it had felt like a thunderstorm between my thighs. I'd never felt anything so powerful, so intimidating ... so *sensual*. But his words, menacing and licking up my spine like poison, were targeted. He meant them, whoever the hell he was.

"Did you get a lot of homework on the first day? How did you prefer Winston?" Bennett walks into the room and zaps my mind out of it's horrible thoughts.

I turn to my soon-to-be stepdad and smile. I guess it was good that if I only got one father figure in this life, it's Bennett. Decked out in his casual attire, which includes a tie and ironed dress pants, his expression is hopeful and open.

Actually, Bennett and I get along quite nicely. I'd never had a father; the low-life had skipped town when Mom had gotten pregnant with me the summer after she graduated high school. Bennett didn't try to parent me, but instead formed a bond with me that I cherished even in the short amount of time we'd known each other. He liked to read, and had introduced me to classics that I hadn't added to my collection. His record albums include The Beatles and Fall Out Boy, so he was okay in my music book. And most of all, he loved my mom as if she was the most rare and precious substance on this earth ... so I'd taken a liking to him instantly.

"I got some light reading and a few question sets for trigonometry, but nothing crazy. And my first day was ... okay." Besides the stares from both students and teachers, and the fact that some British supermodel called me a lamb for slaughter.

Bennett chuckles, taking out some scones from the bread box and putting water in the teapot. "I know some of those kids and professors can be harsh, but know your worth, Nora. You are bloody smart, smarter than any person I know. Focus on that and you'll be okay. Tea?"

Since living in London, I've found that tea and biscuits are the answer to every problem. I'm not sure if I agree, but Bennett does make a mean cup of Earl Grey.

I nod, setting aside the books and papers in front of me. "So, can we finally go to that soccer match you've been promising?"

Before moving all the way across the universe, my mom and I had never done any traveling outside of the East Coast of the United States. It's been Bennett's mission to take us on a grand tour of his country, and his continent. So far, he's shown Mom and I the beautiful gardens at Buckingham Palace, we've spent an afternoon at London Bridge, and a weekend in Italy which I will never forget in my lifetime.

But, he's been bragging about the world's best sport, and I'm anxious to see what the fuss is about.

"First off, it's called football. Bugger, I cringe at that word. And soon, but not this weekend. We have the annual Regents Dinner this weekend, and that will take up most of your mother and I's time. But of course, you'll join us."

He doesn't say it as a command, something I'd feared he'd start doing when we moved to be in his home country. No, he says it as an inclusion, like we are a family and we go together. Kind of like *Grease* or *The Parent Trap*.

But inside, I cringe just like he does at the word soccer. These galas and dinners and royal events are intimidating to say the least, and I no longer look forward to them.

A fake smile plasters to my face, because I need to keep a brave one on for both of them. "Can't wait."

4

NORA

Big red double decker buses zoom down the street, cabs stop for passengers, pedestrians spew onto the sidewalks and streets like a complex maze of bodies.

Having grown up in small town suburbia, I'm completely out of my element in a city. Especially a historic, giant metropolis like London.

Not to say that I don't acknowledge the perks of living here. It is beautiful for one; absolutely breathtaking in both its history and modernity. The culture is unlike anything I've ever experienced, from the theater to the underground scene to the royals. A cult-like exclusive existence that I'm now a part of, I guess.

Bennett escorts my mother from our town car onto the sidewalk, and then reaches back in to offer me a hand. I take it gratefully, and my heels hit the pavement in wobbly unsureness. I guess I need to get used to this if I'm to be attending all of these events now.

Camera flashes blind me, the paparazzi trying to capture any ounce of skin or tension between my mother, Bennett and me. They're vultures in the most basic sense; animals picking the bones of any unsuspecting victim. The hack job they've done on my mother and I has been horrific, and I have to refrain from lifting my middle finger in salute. Wouldn't be very royal of me.

Okay, so technically I'm not a royal and never will be. I'm a side attachment, the bastard as much as Jon Snow is. Half of Bennett's family just tightly nods at me whenever I'm in the room.

The Dunmore Ballroom is lit up like a Christmas tree, with red spotlights and a cream-colored carpet adorning the entrance. It's definitely the grandest affair I've been to since we touched down, and I won't lie and say there aren't enormous moths flapping around in my stomach. I wipe my damp hands on the navy floor-length wrap dress one of the Palace stylists picked out, and pull the silver wrap around my shoulders a little tighter.

Before my future stepdad fell into our lives, jeans and dusty Converse were the norm. Now? I'm adjusting to cashmere, silk and tulle. The dresses they put me in, the hairstyles they whip up, the way in which the experts make my skin look dewy and sharp at the same time. I reach my left hand up self-consciously and finger a soft, red curl.

I have to admit, the pampering has been easy to get used to. For someone who used to swipe on ChapStick and call it a day, the prettiness of it all is alluring. And even though it may be vain, I feel sexy and womanly in a way I never have before.

"*Rachel! Rachel! Will you be wearing the traditional McAlister veil?*"

"*Has Bennett told you about his past?*"

"*Nora! Do you still have that bikini?*"

The slam of reality into my temples is harsh and blinding, and the bodyguards rush us inside.

We're tucked into a corner of the foyer, the maroon and gold carpet as rich as the gold leaf wallpaper. Chandeliers hang from every inch of the ceiling, and someone asks if they can take my wrap.

"Will this ever stop?" I hear my mother whisper to Bennett, who presses his lips to the side of her forehead.

"Unfortunately, as much as I want it to, probably not. This is my life, and I don't know how to apologize for dragging you into it."

Mom sighs but smiles. "You didn't, I dragged myself in. And there is nowhere I'd rather be."

It's as if they only have the capacity to see each other, and even though she is my parent, it's very romantic. I guess I never really believed in love the way they seem to have it, until I saw it between them.

"Duke McAlister, your presence is required in the ballroom, now." A man in a tuxedo appears out of nowhere, looking very official.

And just like that, we all snap to, putting on professional faces. It isn't like I was forced to take a course on etiquette, but with all of the events I've been to in the past three months, I might as well have been.

The rules are numerous and sometimes stuffy. I'm to follow behind my mom and Bennett whenever they enter a room, and none of us can ever touch affectionately in a setting such as this. I'm to excuse myself if I need to get up from the table, and curtsy when the men stand to dismiss me from it. Even though my eighteenth birthday has come and past, I'm only allowed a sip of champagne during a toast, and no more. The salad fork is on the left, higher ranking officials must start a conversation with you and not the other way around, and under no circumstances am I supposed to start a flirtation with anyone. Bennett's advisor, Jasper, was very clear about that.

"This could be fun, kiddo." Mom smiles at me just as we're about to be introduced to the ballroom.

I roll my eyes, showing her my enthusiasm. At least one thing hasn't changed since our lives were turned upside down, and that's the relationship we have. It may be corny, but my mom really *is* my best friend. She's the yin to my yang, the one who will rub my back when I'm sick and open all of the car windows when a good song comes on in the middle of a summer drive.

"Introducing, Duke Bennett McAlister of Westminster, and his fiancée, Ms. Rachel Randolph, accompanied by her daughter, Miss Nora Randolph."

The elaborate, floor to ceiling doors open into the ballroom, and the dazzle of hundreds of twinkling chandelier lights hit my corneas before I process anything else. I try to keep my head straight and my gaze forward, but there are too many things to see. Noble men in the most expensive tuxedos I've ever seen, the women that accompany them in floor length gowns of the most beautiful colors. Tables set with mile high floral arrangements, with china that must have been forged in the early nineteenth century.

From somewhere over our heads, an orchestra plays a pretty but regal tune, and the entire room stands at attention to greet my future stepfather.

Even with all of its intricacies and headaches, this life was mesmerizing. I may complain about the attention and the rumors, but this was every little girl's dream in her deepest heart. I was living a princess's life, and it was moments like this that shook me straight to the core and almost knocked me on my ass.

But just to be sure, I secured my wobbling ankles in my heels. Last thing I needed was the press getting ahold of a story about me falling flat on my face at one of the most important dinners of the year.

After our entrance, we are seated at one of the head tables, and the boring conversations begin. About policy and the government and polo matches. I largely tune it out, picking at the overly dressed Waldorf salad that's been set in front of me.

By the time Bennett starts in about a charity theater project he's heading up, my ears can't take anymore. "Excuse me, I'm going to use the restroom."

I get a couple of blank stares from some around the table, and I realize too late that I've used an American word.

"Okay, honey, you'll be okay on your own?" My mom sets a hand on my mine.

"Of course, Mom, I'm not going to fall in." I whisper this only to her, as bathroom humor doesn't seem like it would be appreciated in this crowd.

Walking across the ballroom, I feel the eyes glued to me. Some stares are greedy, given by men too old to be looking at me like that. Others are inquisitive, wanting to know more about what lies underneath my skin. And others are malicious, wishing me ill will or harm. When you've been stared at the way I have for weeks on end, you get good at gauging the weight of people's glances. Of feeling their intentions simply from the expression they cast upon you.

Once in the foyer, I head for the direction I think the bathrooms may be.

"HA!" A shrieking laugh captures my attention.

But the sound didn't come from the hallway I'm in, rather, it came from above. Moving out from the hallway I've walked down, I spot a staircase, marble and red carpet sweeping up to a floor I can't see.

Another sound comes, this one deeper, more male in its tone.

And I'm too curious not to follow it. The sound of my heels is muffled on the carpet as I use the big sloping bannister to climb.

"Give me some of that!" A girlish lilt trickles out of a

doorway as my foot hits the top step, and a beam of light splashes onto the marble floor.

"Come over here and take it." A boy's voice, laced with innuendo, calls back to her.

"Bloody hell, Ed, this tastes like piss." Another girl's voice, deeper than the first one, rings out.

I move closer, trying to get an eye on the first interesting scene I've come across all night.

But my hand must hit the wall, or my heel makes a scratching noise on the floor, because before I know it, I'm face-to-face with the same pair of condescending green eyes that assaulted me in the hallway on the first day of school.

"Well, well, what do we have here?"

Once again, the fawn stuck in headlights falls right into my crosshairs.

Of course, I knew she'd be attending tonight with her crock of a stepfather and gold-digging mother. I hadn't planned any hijinks or takedowns, but here she was, spying on me and my mates.

Swinging the doors open, I present her grandly to our merry band of drunk spoiled children.

"We have a spy. Or worse, an American."

Speri, one of the girls who has always run in our circles, giggles as she tips the vodka bottle back onto her lips. Katherine and Eloise sneer, fluffing down their own dresses in obvious jealousy. Drake, the prime minister's son, starts to clap and hum the American national anthem. Ed laughs, but I see his eyes roaming over her in obvious interest.

And I can't fault him for that, even though anger simmers in my blood at the thought that my cock finds this peasant appealing. She's a nobody, a commoner, and yet when she swishes her hips a little, backing up in surprise, my other head perks up, coming to life as the navy material of her dress catches the light from the room behind me.

"Oh come off it, Asher, invite her in. She can be our play thing, plus she's probably as bored as we are." Drake winks at her, and the girl's eyes go wider than the English Channel.

"Yeah, maybe we can get her drunk and make her sing country songs." Katherine snorts, a sound that is unattractive coming from her thin lips. But as the Duke of Manchester's cousin, she has a place here, and I can't risk blowing her off.

I turn back to her, and hold out a hand while flashing her a wolfish smile. "You heard them, come on in. If you dare."

My challenge seems to light something in her, and embers flare in her irises. "Nora Randolph, although clearly you already know who I am. Which says more about my status than yours, since I have absolutely no idea who any of you are."

Nora slaps a palm into my own, taking the handshake that was only offered as a sign of intimidation. Behind us, Ed whistles and laughs, saying something about how this girl is brilliant.

The minute our hands connect, a sizzle of electricity races down my spine, landing with a jolt squarely in my balls. The creamy porcelain of her soft skin molds with my larger hand, a hand that could crush her delicate body if I so chose. Nora's eyes lock onto mine like a heat-seeking missile, looking for any crack in the defense.

I assess just the same, scanning her flawless face, the wisps of fiery red falling down onto her shoulders. The way her dark, murky eyes, the color of Earl Grey tea, spark. How her cheek bones seem to angle up with her chin, both distinct and defiant in their repugnance of me. I let it be known that my eyes are moving down, my brows lifting in challenge as I move over her small but perky breasts. A mouthful if that, but put together so nicely in her party dress. Her frame is small, almost tomboyish at first glance, but I've seen the bikini pictures. And I'm a man, I can imagine what it would be like to have her bare, under me.

"You don't scare me, Nora," I whisper, using my grip on her hand to pull her marginally closer. "And you're not fooling anyone. If we wanted you to know who we were, we would have introduced ourselves. But I'll give you one, since you're playing a losing game. I'm Asher Frederick, and you may not know my family, but trust me, you want to be scared of me."

A giggle sounds from behind us as Eloise clears her throat. "Asher's family is ace at manipulating people into doing what they want them to do."

I give her another devious smile and drop her hand, much to the dismay of my semi. "Please, your highness, come on in."

"Princess of the trailer park is more like it." Speri hiccups.

I back up, turning from Nora and making my way over to a leather wingback chair. The place we've taken over at this stuffy event is some kind of conference room. But in true British fashion, it isn't without its roaring fireplace and first edition war manuscripts.

"I'm going to go ..." Her unfamiliar accent touches my ears.

"Oh, my arse ... back to where? That bloody awful ballroom so old farts can talk about the good ole days? Stay here, beautiful, and let us corrupt you." Ed gets up and makes his way over to her, shoving a liquor bottle in her hand.

Katherine and Eloise sit spinning an empty beer bottle between themselves on the table, laughing every time it lands on one of them.

I hear the clack of heels, and know she is moving farther into the room. I keep my back turned, eyes to the fire. Her challenging words and little lost fawn expression are affecting me more than I want them to.

"I don't drink." She sets the bottle on the table with a clank, and I presume settles into a chair. The give of old leather betrays her.

Drake laughs. "Bugger, that's depressing. It's the only way we all manage to get through these smashing soirees. That or shagging."

Eloise laughs at that. "Rubbish, everyone knows you're still a virgin."

"She's lying, darling. Unless that's your thing, in which case, I've just been waiting for an angel like you."

"No thanks, I'm not into British assholes."

Nora's words make me finally turn around, because she's being a tosser and thinks she has an upper hand.

"And here I thought she was a slag. But apparently she only likes bloody Americans." I look around the room, making sure everyone laughs at my joke.

See, this isn't the extent of our group, but we are the best of them. The ones who get invited by proxy to these dinners, ceremonies, political events, grand openings. Our parents and relatives are the ones who hold the most power, who are the cream of the crop when it comes to invitation lists. And I am the ring leader, the one who herds and grooms the pack. If someone isn't doing something I like, they need to be reminded to fall in line.

Like Eloise said, I'm very good at manipulation.

My friends laugh at my ribbing of Nora, but the poor girl just doesn't get it.

"A slag?" She looks bored, and I want to punch a wall.

"Slut. Whore. Easy lay. Good time girl. You know, kind of like Katherine," Eloise chimes in helpfully.

Speri laughs and Katherine hits Eloise quite hard on the arm.

And by the way Nora's cheeks pink up, I can tell she is none of the above. But it feels brilliant to embarrass her.

"You can join in on the game if you want to." Katherine lifts an eyebrow at her, and Drake moves to stand near the table too.

"In fact, I think we should all join the game." Ed takes a swig from the scotch bottle he's been nursing.

My veins are relatively clear of alcohol, even though I'd been slowly sipping a glass of Macallan over the past hour and a half.

"Spin the bottle? How passé. Let's go to a club or something instead," Speri whines.

"While I'd love nothing more, dear old dad would go mental if I left. Plus, I want to spend some time with our new friend." Drake's eyes flash, and I know what he's thinking.

To be honest, I'd rather go cause some mischief out at a club, but this seems like a better idea.

Nora looks so out of her element, it's laughable. "Isn't that for grade schoolers? We aren't twelve."

Her words hold sarcasm but her eyes tell a different story. She's scared and uncomfortable, and I want to push all of those buttons.

"Since I'm apparently twelve, I guess I'll go first." Ignoring her comment, I step up to the table and spin.

The bottle vibrates on the old wood tabletop, spinning round and around as one of the girls giggles and Ed hoots. The seconds seem to tick by in slow motion, and I can feel Nora's eyes on the back of my neck. Feel the electricity humming between us. Smell her fear and anticipation.

So slowly that it feels as if we're moving through molasses, the vodka bottle stops, pointing across the room.

Directly at Nora.

"There it is then, poppet. Pucker up, shall we?" I wear the smile of a panther about to trap its prey.

Her posture stiffens, those slim arms giving a subtle shake as the quiver of arousal, if I'm not mistaken, travels down her spine.

And then, for the second time in a week, Nora Randolph

turns on her heel and bolts away from me. My friends break out into a rash of laughter, making kissing noises, and even Drake pats me on the arse.

I let her go, knowing it's the last time I'll allow her to save herself.

One of the questions the press often asks of me, or shouts at me at a distance, is if I miss my home. I typically brush it aside with some general cliché, or no answer at all ... but what I should say is that you'd have to feel a part of something to actually miss it.

The truth is, there wasn't much of a life for me to leave behind when Bennett asked my mom and I to follow him halfway across the world. Because of my gift, I was a relative outsider, even to the people in the town I'd called home my whole life. Weird, strange, off, ill ... these labels were slapped on me as if I was a reject toy coming off of the assembly line.

Our house in Pennsylvania was a home because it had Mom and I, but in reality, I didn't have any friends. There wasn't anyone else I turned to, not even a supportive teacher or guidance counselor or old shoe store clerk who would give me sage wisdom. I was as much a nobody there as I am here ... only now I'm surrounded by cryptic talking rich people with sophisticated British accents.

The sweat that has collected on my brow at facing another class, worrying if I'll see any of the six faces from that library on

Saturday night, trickles onto my eyelash. So far, I've only seen the girl that Asher called Katherine, and I think she was too drunk to remember my face. Thank goodness. I'd begun to think I'd dreamed the upstairs portion of Saturday night.

"Blimey, this day just keeps getting better."

My determination to stare straight down at my notebook is zapped as my head snaps up to look at the person sliding into the desk on my right. The fair-haired boy from Saturday night, the one with blazing blue eyes and a set of charming dimples etched into his cheeks, is looking right at me with a smarmy smile on his perfectly symmetrical face.

"I don't believe we were properly introduced. I'm Drake Coddington." He extends his hand as if I'm supposed to shake it with gratitude.

Wait a second. "Coddington as in Prime Minister Albert Coddington?"

I didn't mean to say that out loud, but the thought popped into my head so fast that my mouth didn't cooperate. While preparing for the move, I'd read countless books on the British government, Parliament, the Royals ... all to associate myself with the culture I would be immersed in.

"The one and only, that's my pop. But don't ask for an autograph or anything, that would be *so* American of you." To his credit, Drake winks and makes me feel on the inside of a joke for the first time since I've been here.

Not like I was considering it or anything ... okay maybe for a minute. I had a thing for government officials.

"Such a shame you had to leave so quickly on Saturday, we were having so much fun." He twists his green and blue plaid tie around his finger in such an effortlessly sexual way that I realize I'm drawn to the motion.

"I didn't want to invade on you and your friends, like I'd

said." And his friend Asher had confused my body and mind more than anyone I'd ever met, but I wasn't about to say that.

"You are one of us now, love. Better get used to it, or you'll never have any fun." His expression, guilty and playful all at the same time, told me exactly how much fun he wanted to have.

I squirmed in my chair, wishing the professor would walk in and start class soon. All around me, students were filing in, chatting or checking their smartphones. Winston was a world of its own, with social rules and a hierarchy that mimicked my high school in Pennsylvania, but were amplified to the tenth degree. Where kids back home had pickup trucks, Winston kids had drivers and Rolls Royces. Where we had Home Economics and English, they had Etiquette class and 19th Century Romantic Novelists. Where we had Lucky Brand jeans and Forever 21 crop tops, they had Chanel, Dior and Prada.

I wasn't one of them, and I never would be. So I changed the subject. "You're a senior, right? What do you have lined up for next year?"

It seemed a safe bet, since everyone around the academy was buzzing about university acceptances. I'd applied to a few US and UK schools, but it would be months before I heard anything.

Drake rolled his eyes. "The only thing I'm looking forward to next year are parties, but I get enough of those now so how fun can university be. I've already been accepted to Oxford, same as Asher."

Of course they'd already been given the key to the golden gates ... the top of the top. "Well that must be nice, having a friend there when you go to college."

Drake chuckles, one blond brow rising. "Oh you poor thing, you don't get it. Let me fill you in; people of our stature don't have friends. We have allies and enemies. Those who have the most power stick together, take up for each other with our steel armor and quick swords of manipulation. And our enemies ... well, let's just say they are left quivering in their own poverty. This isn't the suburbs of wherever you came from, this is the grand event. Either walk over the weak's bodies, or fall to the bottom with them."

I sucked in a breath at his bluntness, because the sheer, cruel honesty of these people still caught me off guard. In America, we glossed things over, putting on a smile and a wink while we went behind your back. Or at least ... people who did that kind of stuff did. I was finding that in London, they came straight out with their verbal assaults and fear mongering, they had no time for pleasantries or two-facedness. It was both refreshing and terrifying.

"I'll ... keep that in mind." Not that I ever planned to step over anyone's body, but it would be wise to keep my cards close.

"Good." He reached over to pat my hand as if I was a school child he'd just taught a lesson. "Now that that's learned, I'm inviting you on our trip to Paris this weekend. And before you say no, just know that I won't allow it. So simply, darling, say yes."

The professor for our Human Biology and Anatomy course walks in, clapping his wrinkly old hands to quiet the chattering students.

Drake's advice about allies and enemies rings in my head, and I think that maybe it's just about time I started weighing the positives of following his suggestion. All my life, I've stayed in the background, settled for being the girl who quietly went about her business in the shadows and didn't try to rise above the hand she was dealt.

But now I'd been dealt another hand. And that allows me to lean over, making eye contact with Drake, and mutter yes before the lesson begins.

"**I**'m home!"

My words echo off of the big front entry way to our residence in Kensington Palace, and I forget again that those words sound different when the people in the house probably can't even hear you. And to my assumption, no one answers.

I hang my coat up in the closet and place my backpack on the floor, taking out the textbooks I need to do my homework for the night. I know that there is a whole staff of people to clean up after us, but it is still something I can't get used to. I don't need people to do things for me when I'm perfectly capable of doing them myself.

Making sure everything is neatly put away, I go off in search of any living soul I might find.

Ten minutes later, I find my mom in the study upstairs. "Hi, Mama."

She instantly looks up, her smile radiating through me. "Hi, sweetness. How was your day?"

You'd think that after the hours of events she puts in all week, she'd look exhausted. But as usual, my mom looks fresh faced and incredible. She'd had me when she was eighteen, and as an eighteen-year-old now, I could never imagine doing what she'd done. Even after the asshole who'd helped create me abandoned her, she'd loved me more than humanly possible and provided as best as she could. It may go against every other angsty teenage girls' thoughts, but my mom was my hero.

"It was good. I feel like I'm being challenged more, so I guess that's a good thing."

I had always kept my answers about school very nonchalant, very typical-kid responses. Even when we lived in Pennsylvania, I never wanted her to be stressed about what was happening with me at school. So, especially now, I didn't want to give her anymore to pile onto her plate.

"That's so great, honey, I'm glad you're adjusting more. Lord knows you'll get a better education here than you ever would have back home. Although, you'd excel anywhere, I know that. Oh, man ..."

Mom looks down at the laptop propped on her lap, the velvet green arm chair capsizing her in its largeness. It's funny, I never thought my mom quite looked right anywhere in our small town, but here? The elegant decor, the jewels, the gowns, the prestige ... she just *fit*.

But being the fiancée, and soon-to-be wife, of a future king was hard work. She was working sixty hours a week with the schedule they had her on, more than her job at the diner back home. Appearances, charity events, etiquette classes, lessons on the government, ribbon cuttings, anything that she had to do to please the people of Great Britain, she was doing it.

"Mom, maybe you need to slow down?" I knew she wouldn't, but I had to say something.

She smiled wearily, pushing the same red hair that matched my own over her shoulder. "I'm happy to do this if it makes it easier on Bennett."

Of course she was, and in a way, I didn't blame her. If he didn't see what a sacrifice she was making for him, I would have protested. But I knew how much he loved and adored her.

I didn't want to add one more thing to her plate, but I found that I wanted to go to Paris. Desperately. Drake had lit that idea of freedom in me like a low blazing spark, and it was slowly eroding my insides.

"So ... school was so good this week that I actually got invited to hang out with some classmates this weekend ..."

At that, she shuts her laptop, the sound reverberating off the oak-paneled walls. "Really?! Honey, that is awesome!"

Now for the tricky part. "Yeah ... well, you know these type of people, Mom, and well, this group of friends invited me to go to Paris for the weekend—"

Mom cuts me off before I can even try to throw out lame excuses. "Um, what? Paris? You're joking, right? You think I'm going to let my eighteen-year-old go to a foreign country with a bunch of peers for the weekend? Dream on, toots."

Annoyed for her in a teenager way I probably never had been before, I rolled my eyes. "It's not a foreign country, it's practically a state next door! And come on, this is me we are talking about. I'm responsible, reliable. I'm sure Bennett has eyes all over that area, and I'll check in every hour."

I'm all but stamping my foot and slamming my bedroom door. I can see her hazel eyes start to soften, and I know I've planted a seed of doubt in her brain.

"Come on, Mom. This is a great opportunity for me. I'll see a new city, be able to make some friends. Really branch out for the first time in my life." And now the guilt came in ... I couldn't believe I was playing the card but the words were tumbling out. "We moved here so you could follow your dreams, and your love. And I love that, I love you ... but you have to let me have my own dreams and freedom too."

Sympathy and guilt cloud her eyes and I know I have her. I feel a bit slimy for playing her like this, but I want to go. For the first time since we got here, and maybe in my life, I actually have a niggling interest in doing something with kids my own age.

"Okay ... fine. But you keep the tracking on your phone, and one of Bennett's bodyguards is going with you."

In a weirdly rare moment for me, giddiness bubbles up through my throat and out in a screech as I hug my mother. I've never been the excitable, boy-crazy, hair flipping teenage girl ... and I'm not really going to start now. But, in this moment, I get the excitement that used to wash over my high school classmates when they talked about prom or Friday night football games.

What did one even pack for a trip to Paris? While I didn't need people to do things for me, I could admit when I was defeated. And fashion was definitely one of the areas that stumped even my brain.

It was time to call in the professionals.

Push, pull. _Burn, relief. Sink, stroke._

The ache in my muscles was one I craved, the mindless action of my body a thing I lived for. This was something I knew inside and out; an activity I was bloody good at without having to try or concentrate at all.

Although most things in my life were like that.

The coxswain yelled out commands, but I barely registered his orders. I knew the timing, the depth of the oar, the speed of which the waves were coming. My motions were fluid and precise, dead on with the other members of my rowing team.

I'd been in the water since I could walk, and the minute I'd been eligible, my father had signed me up for the only sport dignified enough to qualify under his standards. Rowing was a distinguished sport, an activity that could be viewed during sunny London afternoons where posh people watched from the banks and then enjoyed a glass of bubbly after.

"Rowing to China, eh, mate?" Winston, one of the teammates I've come up through the ranks with, nudges me with his foot as we continue to glide effortless through the water.

I snap out of the trance I'm in, not even having realized I was furiously putting my all into it. "Shut up, wanker."

"Oh come on, you don't need to exert that much effort, Frederick." He laughs, missing a beat with his oar.

"And that's why your family is just beneath the upper crust. An attitude like that will get you nowhere." I grunt out the dig.

He makes a muffled, pissed off sound, and I feel ashamed for a minute. The slimy grief that sludges through my veins for that backhanded comment weighs me down, until it slides right off my back. It's what I do, my method for everything. Bully, manipulate, belittle ... I learned from the best. It comes so second nature to me; my soul must be as black and burnt as an ashen volcano by now.

The boat reaches its destination point, and everyone relaxes, ceasing the furious motions we were just completing in sync. My body burns, my calves and biceps roar with exertion. But it feels good, cathartic, to release all of the pent-up frustration inside of me.

This week has been a notch above hell, with schoolwork and my father on my back, piling up the demands day after day. The knowledge of Bennett's betrayal, which weighs heavier on me each second of my life, pounds on my temples like a hammer. Seeing glimpses of Nora in the hall, in the courtyard, getting into her car ... I want to approach her again but I need her to come to me this time. To seek it out.

I don't linger to talk with my teammates, most of whom I don't attend school with. Some of them have already moved on to university, and others are in different private schools around London. I head for the bathhouse, wanting the showers to myself before the animals descend.

As the hot, soapy water makes its way over my abs and still aching thighs, my thoughts drift to the plan. The one I'd set in motion months ago, to once and for all disgrace the man who'd killed my mother.

If it wasn't for my father, when he was on the piss and stumbling around like a wounded animal, I would never have known that my mother died for any other reason than it was her time. At first, it was just ramblings. He would sit in his study at night, me as a child sitting by the fire playing with my train set.

"She was murdered ... he took her ... he'll pay."

As I got older, I understood what his knackered diatribes were about, the person responsible for my mother being behind the wheel the night she went over the side of London Bridge that night ten years ago.

Wiping my brain of the cobwebs of terrors past, I dried off and changed. I had a plane to catch, and it just so happened that Paris for the weekend was exactly what I needed.

Thirty minutes later and I'm pulling my Aston Martin onto a private runway, where a gleaming white jet awaits with its stairs waiting to take my friends and I up and away.

"How come when I get an auto, you always get a posher one?" Ed slams the door of his red Ferrari, which is too obvious for my taste.

As the steward grabs my luggage and takes it to the plane, I fall into step beside him. Patting his cheek, I find I'm in a rather chipper mood. "Mate, you haven't come to that reality yet?"

"Psh, whatever. I'm going to see some French birds tonight and at least that will ease my pain. We better be staying at your father's flat, that place is bloody brilliant."

His pain, *yeah* ... the guy had never suffered in his life. By most folk's standards, neither had I.

"Quit being a desperate git ... but yes, we're staying there. Now get on the plane."

We boarded, Ed taking a minute too long to check out the pretty flight attendant. I smack the back of his head, nudging him down the aisle. The beige leather and polished wood of the cabin comes into view, and there is already an entire bar set up between the chairs on the right side. Soon, Katherine and the rest of the girls come along in a gaggle, toting the stench of perfume and too-large handbags with them.

"Can someone confirm that Privé is open tonight? If not, I'm not sure why we're even going to Paris ..." Eloise rolls her eyes and settles into her seat, sipping the flute of champagne someone brought over.

"It is, my connection texted me." Katherine waved her phone in the air. "Hope you brats brought your A game."

Ed clapped his hands surreptitiously, and I continued to stare out the window. I was the least excitable out of my group of friends, but even I had to admit that there was something uniquely special about a night out at Privé. The ultra-exclusive club, literally meaning private in French, was so hard to find, you needed a special map and key to get in. We'd been a couple of times before, so I knew from firsthand knowledge that the entrance was inside a department store in the main district of Paris, with a key code combination. From the outside, the door looked like an employee stock room entrance, but once you were in ...

"Hope we're not too late to the party!" Drake walks through the cabin, and I can't make out the person behind him.

"It's just like you, mate, to bring an unauthorized date—"

I start to talk, but am cutoff mid-sentence when I see Nora walking up the aisle. Her scarlet hair is windblown, the white dress floating around her body sets off the peachy tones of her skin. She looks like some kind of country princess, and I have to chuckle to myself because she pretty much is exactly that.

"I hope y'all don't mind, I brought a friend. She's never been to Paris before, so we have to show her a good time."

Everyone is silent, assessing the newcomer like she might

bite. Nora chews on her bottom lip, and I find my cock lengthening with the need to bite it myself. It must be the hatred toward her fueling my arousal. Typically, I regard females like playthings, discarding them after one or two uses. I've never thought seriously about a woman in my life, and I wasn't about to start now.

"Have a glass of champagne, new girl." Speri holds out a flute and the tension seems to be broken. For now.

Nora sits down by the girls and begins to chat, about what I can't hear. I'm too far away and trying to keep my distance. Like I said, she has to come to me. The plane takes off, the ascent seamless as the sun descends over London. I could shut my eyes and nap a spot, knowing we'll be up until four in the morning at the club, but I'm too energized by our late arrival's presence.

"I brought along the one you fancy, just for you." Drake sits across the aisle, his button down rolled up at the sleeves as he leans over with a wolfish smile.

I don't tear my eyes from the window. "What would make you think I have any remote interest in her?"

"Because you ignored her when she walked on to this plane. You always ignore the ones you want. You may not think I know much about you, Asher Frederick, but I see all."

Annoyance tics in my jaw, knowing that he recognizes a tell of mine. So I play it off in my favor. "I just see those virgin lips and go crazy, you know she's untouched."

With a satisfied smile, Drake swills the dark liquor in his glass. "Amen to that, mate."

The rest of the flight goes without complications, but whenever I look to where Nora sits farther up the cabin, her eyes dart away. Almost like she was watching to see if I'd look. Almost as if she wanted me to.

Oh, how fun this trip was going to be.

I'd gotten in over my head.

Who the hell did I think I was? Who was that girl at school earlier this week who'd had all the confidence of a seven-foot NBA player?

Because she certainly wasn't here now.

First of all, this was only my fourth time on an airplane in my life, and I'd forgotten how deathly scared I was of the takeoff and landing. Good thing most of the popular crowd was drunkenly napping when we landed, or they would have been able to see the white flesh of my knuckles digging into the plush leather.

I'd purposely gotten myself into this situation, thinking that a trip to Paris with new faces would bring me closer to some destiny that I'd always secretly dreamed of. What bullshit.

Instead, I'd forgotten that Asher was one of Drake's best friends, that he was going to be here on the plane and invading every second of my trip. I'd forgotten that I wasn't one of these spoiled rich kids, that I wasn't accustomed to private planes or thousand-dollar champagne or secret night clubs. I was going in blind, and I was the type of girl who always needed to see, and see clearly.

Speri pulled a magenta dress from her Louis Vuitton trunk. "Maybe I'll do this one tonight, although I feel like it screams Vegas."

Katherine admired the slinky number her friend held up to her body. "No, the one time you *could* get away with that is in Paris. I say bring it on."

I sat on the bed, outfitted in silk and velvet bedding, watching them discard priceless gowns on the floor as they decided against them. The room was two times bigger than our whole house back in Pennsylvania, and the apartment was one of the flashiest places I'd ever been in. I'm sorry, flat. Two people had already corrected me in the hour we'd been here.

"Fancy any of these, Nora?" Eloise pointed to the material all over the floor, as if I might need help picking something out.

She'd been the nicest of all of them so far, trying to sparingly include me in conversations. Maybe it was because she hadn't always been one of them either. Her father had recently come into fame on the small screen, being cast late in life as one of the main characters on Britain's favorite Thursday night TV show. Her family had moved from working class Liverpool to the first zone of London, and her life had changed just as rapidly as mine was now. Not that she would talk about it or show that vulnerability, but I'd researched each of them a bit after that night in the library.

"Actually, the staff at the palace helped me a little ... since my sense of fashion is absolute crap." I went to my own suitcase and unzipped it, rifling through the clothes.

"Bitch," Katherine laughed, and my head shot up. "Oh, darling I mean that in the best possible way. I have personal shoppers and stylists, but what it must be like to have the palace staff on retainer. Even I can admit jealousy."

"But watch out before she plunges a stiletto into your back." Speri winks at me, although I kind of think she's half-joking.

I smile unsurely, but pull out an emerald green halter dress that when put on, hits me just above the knee. "I was thinking this ..."

The material is as silky as melted butter, and the hue goes well with my red hair. It leaves my freckled shoulders bare, and the majority of my back is visible. But the front is buttoned up, hiding the mediocre chest I do have. The stylist I'd worked with had told me it was "just enough hint of sex" for Paris. Thank God my mother hadn't heard that.

The three girls turn to me as I hold it up, scrutinizing it.

"That will look bomb on you, bitch." Katherine rolls her eyes and goes back to putting her makeup on in the big bright Hollywood mirror at the vanity in the corner.

"I think we need to start drinking." Speri goes to the glass and gold bar sitting along one wall and pours herself a glass of clear liquid.

Before I came to London, I'd never had a sip of alcohol in my life. While most of my classmates had been going to keg parties in the farm fields on the outskirts of town, I'd been at home reading or watching movies with my mom. It had never interested me, and neither had they. But now, with the crew I'd be with tonight, I finally felt that peer pressure I'd always been warned about in high school health class. The champagne on the plane hadn't been bad, although the fizziness in my nose had almost made me sneeze.

"Here, drink up. We have a couple of hours before we go out anyway." Eloise handed me a glass of the same thing she'd prepared herself, and I looked at the clock.

"It's already nine o'clock." When the heck were we actually going to leave?

Katherine chuckled as she smeared smoky black eyeshadow

across her lid. "You're like an alien, I love it. You typically can't go out until eleven, but it's bloody lame to show up when everyone shows up, so we usually wait until twelve."

The rest of the girls brush this off like it's completely normal that we aren't going to this ultra-exclusive nightclub, as teenagers no less, until literally the start of tomorrow. I keep my mouth shut and sit on the bed, watching them flit around with hair tools and palettes of expensive looking makeup.

"Maybe I'll see Jon George there again." Speri curls a lock around the wand she's using in her hair.

Katherine and Eloise start to laugh, and I smile in unison, wanting to act like I'm part of the conversation. At least this girl time is taking the edge off my nerves about Asher. I sip the cranberry and something concoction that Eloise made me and feel the alcohol invade my bloodstream.

"Wasn't his dick small though?" Katherine doesn't even bat a mascara-covered eyelash when she says this.

I however, almost choke on my drink.

"It was okay, bigger than some but smaller than others. But he had a great house in Santorini." Speri shrugs.

Katherine turns to me. "Last time we went to Privé, Speri hooked up with this French millionaire who owns a bloody brilliant house in Greece. She spent like two weeks lounging in his pool and eating his caviar. Are you going to like ... put anything on?"

She points around her own face, indicating the flawlessly crafted look she'd painted on.

"I'm not very good with makeup to be honest ..." And I didn't own anything past the Maybelline mascara and Clinique lipstick I'd swiped on.

"We can teach you! I've got all of the newest MAC stuff, and Katherine's dad practically owns stock in Estée Lauder and Stella." Eloise claps her hands.

I didn't know what those were either ... but I nodded. "I think I'm good for tonight, the dress and heels are enough for me. I'll probably just hang back."

"Oh, hell no, we are getting you pissed and snogged!" Speri jumped onto the bed in front of me.

I didn't like the sound of either, and I was starting to feel uncomfortable with the conversation. "I'm just gonna go grab a water."

Escaping the room before any of them could protest, I slipped into the hallway. Apparently, the flat was in Asher's family, and the way it was decorated, I swear it had cost a fortune and a half. Sleek and modern in a way that screamed sensuality but also exuded that upper crust sensibility that everything the Frederick's did screamed.

Walking into the black and white kitchen, faint red accents dotting every surface from the blender to the microwave, I head for the fridge. I need to flood my body with water if I'm going to try and drink with these professional partiers tonight. As it is, the drink Eloise made me is already buzzing under my skin and making my head float.

"Oh my God!" Just as I close the fridge, a figure is waiting on the other side of the door, making me jump.

"You're in another person's flat, don't be so surprised when they're around." Asher smirks at me, knowing full well that he meant to scare me.

"Don't do some creepy scary movie crap to an unsuspecting victim and maybe I'll remember that." I give him a stink eye and curse myself, because it isn't my smoothest comeback but he makes me nervous. Not that I'd ever admit that to him.

"Oh, I am aware that you're an unsuspecting victim, and believe me, that's what I like about you, Nora."

I'm not sure what it is, but it always feels as if the heat has been turned up a hundred degrees whenever Asher and I occupy the same space. If I touched him, would sparks erupt? It feels like it, the way my belly clenches and beads of sweat collect at the back of my neck. The way his jaw ticks with mischief, the way his emerald eyes burn with sarcasm, the way his tall, lean body ripples with dominance ... I should be running the other way. But instead I stay, waiting to see what barb he'll hit me with next.

I've never been this intrigued and weary of a person at the same time.

The alcohol in my system is also giving me false bravado, and I feel that girl in the classroom with Drake coming back. "Stop being the big bad wolf, *Asher*. It doesn't look very dignified."

I'm not sure how fast or how smoothly he does it, but when I look up again, his chest is nearly touching my own. "Dignified men have been known to do some very undignified things."

He says it as if his tongue is licking up my body, the sex coming off of those words is lethal. He makes the word dignified sound downright dirty. And that's where he gets me, the one chink in my armor.

"I'm going to get ready, try to stay away from me tonight." His teasing knocks me back a step, I'm not used to this overt sexual energy he radiates.

"Make sure you save me a dance, *princess*."

The endearment sounds more like an insult, a jab at how much I am *not* the title I am about to gain.

But when he says the dance in conjunction to both of us, my blood heats to the point of overflowing.

usic pulses from every surface, bouncing the entire club as I lean against a wall in the VIP area.

The ice cubes in my gin and tonic jump with the rhythm, sloshing as I tip it to my mouth and empty the entire thing.

Privé is on another level tonight, and I think the entire club feels it. I know I feel it, with my fourth drink swimming happily in my veins. I lost Drake somewhere in the fray, after we'd all gotten in. Typically, we'd sail past the door, even at our young age ... bouncers everywhere knew who we were. But Nora had cocked it up, making us vouch for her in a very lame fashion. Yet another strike against her.

Ed was in sight, all over a blonde on the dance floor as his beer narrowly missed landing all over her skirt. Katherine and Eloise sat farther back, in the lounge area done in deep purples and aqua lighting. From the drowsy, amused looks on their faces I could tell they were rolling on ecstasy, a sleazier looking bloke who had to be the dealer sitting next to them. Speri had already gone home with her latest conquest, finding him only an hour into our night. Who knew if we'd see her again in the next week.

The exclusive club was one big rectangle, but it was cordoned off. In the center was a giant dance floor, with aqua and blue lights swimming overhead, giving it an underwater illusion. On the far wall was a gigantic metal bar stocked with all of the top shelf liquor on the market, and other bottles that only people in our stratosphere had ever heard of or drank. The lounge area where the girls sat was next to the bar; low velvet couches and sunken armchairs created a sexy, relaxed vibe. And then all over the club were hidden corners and drapes that fell from the ceiling, creating hideaways where one could get into trouble.

"Hi, handsome." A tall, thin brunette assesses me, toying with the straw in her drink between her lips. She's gorgeous, of course, but far too obvious for my tastes.

What most people don't know about me, because I never talk about women, is that I want the chase. I crave it. Girls who throw themselves at me, because that's basically what this type A model is doing, don't get my rocks off.

No, I want the girl who will give me the cold shoulder nine times out of ten. And then the tenth time get on her knees and peek those pretty eyes up at me as I use her mouth in whichever ways I please. That's what gets me hard as a steel pipe.

"Having a good night?" I nod at her, my expression as unchanging as my position is. I may not be interested, but I can see a certain figure from the corner of my eye watching our interaction.

Plus, I've had four drinks and am more pliable to situations than I normally am.

"It would be better if you would dance with me." She bats those long, and probably fake, eyelashes at me.

Yeah, not going to happen. The other thing I don't do is dance, regardless of what I told Nora before.

"Sorry, love, not tonight. I'm keeping it low key." I give the slightest nod of my head, indicating sympathy when in reality I have none.

"Oh, come on, you know you want to." The brunette twists her body, giving me more of a view.

And here is where the asshole comes out. "I tried to be nice, but I'm not interested, at all. You look just like every other wannabe model in this place, and I know that when it comes to fucking you, you're a dime a dozen."

Her jaw drops, and she backs away. "Prick!"

She spits the word before she turns on a heel and marches away. I lean back, the wall acting as my camouflage once again. If I have another drink I'll be stumbling home, but if I don't, the buzz will wear off far too quickly before the night ends.

Casting a glance farther down the wall, I watch Nora sway ever so slightly to the hypnotic techno beat. She's off by herself, almost in the very most corner of the room, away from the crowd and observing each interaction in front of her. From the way she moves, from the half empty drink in her hand, I can tell she's drunk.

As the lights illuminate her body, searching like beams in the night sky, I can't help but fully turn my head. That dress, the deepest color green, has me greedy. It molds to her form as if it's a second skin, showing me all of the petite curves that my hands itch to touch. Just knowing I can't unwrap that package has me hardening in my trousers.

Her hair tumbles around her shoulders like fiery lava; I may get burned if I wrap my fist in it, but bugger do I want to try. And she's done something different to her eyes and cheeks tonight. The natural look she usually sports does a lot to my growing cock, but tonight Nora is different. She's amplified, more sexed up with the dark eyelashes and sparkling skin.

Before I devise my next move, my feet are already walking over to where she holds up the wall.

Nora sees me coming, her eyes tracking me with hesitation. But I see the desire behind that stare, the interest and intrigue. When I make it to her, I lean my back on the wall and keep my eyes straight. Will she speak first?

The dominant in me needs her to, to cede power to me.

Electricity pings between us, and I can feel the heat coming off of her elbow, so close to my own. The refusal of touch, of speech, has my balls drawing up tight. She's playing hard to get, the hardest I may have ever seen. I don't think I've ever been more turned on.

"You're so damn weird." Nora snorts.

So surprised, her words wash over me like the fifth drink I never had. "That was not what I was expecting."

She turns her body toward me, and she's so close that the material of her dress almost brushes my fingers.

"I'm really not, that's the thing. I'm not the person everyone is expecting. You barely know me, but what I know about you is so weird. You like to act like nothing affects you, that you're above it all. But come on, Asher, you wouldn't be here if you really didn't care what everyone thought. You wouldn't be following in whatever footsteps it is you so clearly want to traverse. You have friends, but I don't think they're really your friends. And besides that, I know nothing. Yet, you've gone out of your way to terrorize me, intimidate me. And that's what I find weird."

"Terrorize is a strong word." I finally turn my face to hers, and strike her with the best lopsided grin I can give.

It works, as Nora physically steps back, her mouth flitting open and her eyes falling to my own lips. I've surprised her, almost to the point where she can't function because almost a full minute passes before she coughs and meets my eyes.

"You promised you'd save me a dance, duchess." I don't even dance, but right now I'm trollied and horny.

And the girl in front of me is playing all of the right moves. Not that she's playing; she really does think I'm a bloody bastard, I can tell.

"No, thank you." Her nod is curt as she averts those hazel eyes away from me.

But I'm too close now, and rejection was the one thing that made me move closer. "I'm not told no. Ever."

Now her eyes flit up, connecting with mine like flint striking stone. "Well, we all have to learn something new eventually."

Her voice is like ice, and I want so badly to take her by the arms and show her just how much I can teach her. But we're not ready for that, and my plan doesn't allow for callous actions. Nora, the princess that she is, needs to be wooed. I need to fool her into thinking that I've romanced her, make her feel comfortable, adored.

I chuckle like she's actually teaching *me* something. "I guess we do." Sticking out my hand, I bow. "May I request the honor of a dance with your royal highness?"

It's poison in my mouth, using those words in association with a commoner like her.

I see the flicker of a smile cross her peach lips, and I know I've pressed a soft spot. "Oh, come on, you can't hold up the wall all night. It's your first time at a club, you have to immerse yourself."

Nora folds her arms across her chest, ever the sassy one. "And who says it's my first time at a club?"

I hold back a snort. "You've looked uncomfortable ever since we got here. Which is okay, but let me show you some of the finer things in life."

Adding an eyebrow raise, I reach out gently but surely. My fingers spark when they make connection with her elbow, and like a newborn fawn, I lead her out to the dance floor cautiously. Nora resists at first, trying to pull her arm back into her own personal space, but my grip is firm. Her silky, porcelain-colored flesh feels too good under my hand, and the need to control her grows stronger with the drinks in my system.

Reaching the outskirts of the dance floor, I blend us into the crowd, moving her in front of me and forward. We're so close that the back of her head is almost tucked under my chin, her ass swaying desirably near the crotch of my trousers.

"I don't ... know .... how!" Nora screams over the music, her body going rigid as I move us into the fray.

My hands clasp her hips, pulling her all the way back toward me, molding her back to my front. She tenses even more, trying to pull away. In here, with all of the bodies surrounding us, I can't use charm to bend her to my will. So I show her.

Finding the beat of the music, I start to sway our bodies in a tantric motion. Hips back and forth, moving mine and her own, my big hands mechanically matching her rhythm to my own. Ducking my head, I place my lips right next to her ear, breathing on the lobe until I feel the shiver run down her spine. That seems to take some of the worry and drain it from her form, as she becomes more pliable, moves a little on her own.

I remove a hand from her hip, ghosting it up her arm and to her hair, where I wrap a fistful around my fingers. It's just as silky and thick as I imagined it would be. The song changes and with it does our dance, from faster and more frantic, to slow and sensual. I feel it when Nora picks up the undertones, swaying along with me, almost tilting her head back. I sense it when the music sweeps her up, when her body gets lost and submits to the ways I'm moving it.

I duck my head further into her neck, breathing in her scent of honey and shea butter. She smells like innocence and the country, and it makes my cock grow ever harder. Nora can probably feel it, but she's so zoned out on the alcohol and the vibe that I don't think she notices.

My mouth meets her skin, not kissing or tasting but just floating there, toying with the idea of it. I feel her head tilt toward me, almost overshadowing my own face thats practically buried in her neck. I shift, my chin completely aligned with hers, her lips mere inches from my own. I can taste her breath, cranberry and vodka. She stills against me, as if dancing and staring at my mouth are mutually exclusive things that can only be done one at a time. We hover that way for what seems like days, years.

The music changes again, and it's as if the spell is broken.

Nora wrenches away from me, a disgusted, confused look on her face. She bolts, in the direction of where I don't know. I don't follow her.

I've rattled her, and that's good enough for me. Unfortunately, though, my throbbing balls are left lonely and disappointed in the middle of the dance floor.

10

NORA

Even though I didn't grow up in London, the city and I have an uncanny bond. When I walk the streets, unnoticed in my hat and sunglasses, I feel a sense of familiarity in places I've never stepped foot before.

When my mind gets too much for me to take, when the thoughts and theories become all too much, I just walk. I've convinced my mom, Bennett and the palace guards that not enough of the public know me. I get away with a disguise and a tracking device on my cell phone. My mom helped though, demanding that I needed my private time and space. She knows my secret. She knows how trapped inside my own brain I can get.

My feet brought me here, to the colorful row houses of Notting Hill. The simple beauty, the flowering plants and trees, washes over my anxious soul like a soothing balm. I'm faceless here, and I love it. The quiet elegance of London appeals to me, speaks to me in a way that no other place has. I'm finding more and more, with each open-air market or theater district I explore, that I was meant to find this city. Or, it was meant to find me.

Now that my head space is a little less cluttered, my thoughts carry back to a week ago in Paris.

When Eloise had drunkenly sauntered up to the bouncer, my insides had grown sick with dread. Where I came from, only people over twenty-one could even attempt to get into a place like that. The club was so exclusive that I couldn't even see the front door, but she'd just kissed him on the cheek and shimmied inside. After some vouching by the others, I was let in too.

Let in on an experience I would have never had in a million years had my life not turned on a dime four months ago.

The music. The beat. The drinks. The luxury. The privilege.

It was an overload to my senses, trying to take it all in. The two drinks in my system had turned me silly, my limbs feeling fuzzy and happy.

Asher had approached me, first with his typical sullen attitude. And then he toppled me over, flashing that boyish, flirty grin in my direction. I hadn't known what to do, what with the heat swamping low in my belly and my fingers twitching to reach out and feel the gesture on his face.

The way his hands had engulfed my hips, moving them in slow circles exactly how he wanted me. Even now, heat creeps down my neck and races down my spine, making me itch for ... *something.*

I've never felt the way Asher made me feel that night on the dance floor. Like my insides would burn me alive if he didn't touch me. Like the beat would swallow me whole if he removed his hands from my body, if he stopped the slow circle of his hips into my back. When he'd laid his lips on my neck, just skimming the surface, I thought I would combust from the flames licking up my core.

Not realizing how far I've walked until I reach the tube station fully on the other side of the district I'd intended to stay within, I look around me. No one is able to read my thoughts, *obviously*, but I blush all the same.

I shouldn't want him. I shouldn't have let him get that close. The one thing I know for sure about Asher Frederick is that he is no good. And I also know that if I let him in, he could be the one boy who would really be able to ruin me.

"A nd pencils down!" Professor Mullins wraps hard on her desk with a ruler, her favorite method of getting her point across.

My pencil has been down for three minutes and forty-seven seconds, so I've been watching my classmates as they struggle through the pop quiz in Advanced Math Theory. No one seems to be looking back at me except for Asher, who surprisingly transferred into this class four days ago. And simultaneously kicked whoever was sitting behind me out of their seat so that he could take the spot. I could feel his eyes on my back, looking over my shoulder.

His presence unnerved me, but not to the point where I couldn't ace the course. Math, along with almost every subject, had just always made sense to me. You solved a problem to find the answer. It was simple, no emotions or symbolism clouding it.

"Okay, now please pass your papers to the right of you, and you will grade that person's quiz. No cheating, or it will be off to the headmaster's office for you." Her thick Scottish accent was intimidating enough, not to mention her indomitable height.

I went to hand my paper to the petite blond girl sitting to my right, when it was grabbed out of my hand.

"Emma, you take mine, I'll take Nora's." I turned to see Asher wink at me, and my blood boiled.

"You're going to get us in trouble. Give it back." I sounded like a twelve-year-old.

"Don't worry, Mullins loves me. And besides, I need to see just how smart you are, princess. Can't have a bampot in our inner circle."

Fuming, I face forward and focused on the paper that had been set down on my desk. Thus far, no one at Winston knows or has even guessed at my abilities, and I would like to keep it that way. Maybe everyone else had an easy time with the test too, and my correct answers would go unnoticed to Asher.

My hands were beginning to sweat.

"First question ..." Professor Mullins review drowns out behind the whooshing in my ears as my blood pressure skyrockets.

The hairs on my arms stand up as I hear groans and grunts of frustration around the room. Every kid beside me knows they got the first problem, and then the second problem, and so on, wrong ... meanwhile I take a red pen through the quiz in front of me knowing that I've answered each one correctly so far.

"Hmm ..." The sound comes from behind me, and I'm too scared to turn and see the look on Asher's face.

Ten minutes pass as we grade the quizzes, and when we pass them all back, I hear more grunts of failure. My test comes floating in over my shoulder, he couldn't even be mature enough to hand it to me. Each problem has a big red check mark next to it, my answers all completely right. He doesn't write any sarcastic remark or even leave me a smiley face, but I feel the curious glance at my back.

"Maybe you should all be studying harder rather than attending parties and the theater." She gives the room a stern glance. "Who got more than two correct?"

A couple people raise their hands, and so do I, since I still blend in with the crowd.

"And more than five?"

Two of my fellow students put their hands down, but six still remain so I play along too. My heartbeat is in my throat, not knowing when to hedge my bets and lower my arm.

"How about seven correct, anyone get that?"

I play it safe and place my hand back on my desk, my palm sweaty and my thoughts racing. As long as I appear normal, nameless and just one of the crowd, I'm fine. I've spent years of my life hiding my gift, attempting to blend in as just another high school student.

No one's hand is up now, and Mullins makes a clicking sound with her tongue.

"Uh, wait Professor, it seems we have a modest student among us."

I wish a big black hole would open under my desk and swallow me up as Asher opens his big blabbering, enticing lips.

"It seems that Nora here solved all of the problems correctly."

And he's outed me, without even batting an eyelash. When I turn around, my stink eye in full force, he's leaning back in his chair with his long legs crossed hanging out into the aisle. Those green eyes flash with victory, and his strong jaw tics upward with a smarmy grin.

"Well, Miss Randolph, is that true? Why not share it with us? Your classmates could use a little friendly competition, well done." Professor Mullins tips her beakish nose at me and shares that night's homework, before dismissing the class for the day.

But no one is listening. All around me, stares ranging from mysticism to jealousy are targeted right at my body. The looks of wonder, the distaste, the annoyance ... I'm all too familiar with it. When people find out just what I am, their whole opinion of me changes, the way they regard me flips in an instant. My heart drops, knowing that I no longer have my shield of normality.

As everyone gets up to leave, the silence is broken and they begin to walk out with friends or chat in groups. I take my time, collecting my books slowly and waiting until I'm the last person to walk out.

"So, you didn't want to let anyone in on the fact that you're a genius?"

His accent hits my ears as I'm halfway down the hall, and I can't help but shrink even more into myself. My feet keep moving, ignoring the fact that he's gaining on me.

"Nora, don't take it so personally, there are a lot of smart kids here. We'll still think of you as the commoner, if that's what you're worried about."

Asher's sarcastic jabs only succeed in making me cringe more, because these are labels I've never wanted to carry. Turning swiftly around the corner, I head up the wood-paneled main entrance hall and straight for the doors leading to the courtyard. I have to get out of here.

But before my hand can push the door open, fingers lock around my elbow. "Bloody Christ, would you just wait?"

"Get off of me!" I swat his hand away, tears threatening to spill.

Shit, crying in front of this guy is the *last* thing I need, but he's pushing every button that lights up my anxiety meter.

"I was just joking." Asher shrugs as if he hasn't just cut me off at my knees. It's ridiculous how he fills out the uniform that every other male in this school seems to fade into the background in. I try not to notice.

Rage burns through every pore. "You were just *joking*? Do you have any idea what you just did? As if it's not bad enough I'm the new kid, that people gossip about me every day for being the new gold digging queen's bastard daughter, you have to go and expose my abilities to them? Who gave you that right? You could have kept your mouth shut, done me a solid, helped someone out for once in your pathetic, spoiled life. But you couldn't do that, right, Asher? Manipulation and one-upping is the name of your game, and I shouldn't forget that. Thanks for revealing your true colors, I'll remember them next time."

Halfway through my meltdown, he actually has the decency to look truly stricken. But I don't stay to listen to any bullshit explanations.

My brain has already extended itself enough today, and I feel a migraine coming on. I retreat before the full attack pulls me into its dark abyss, too paranoid to let Asher see another one of my differences.

ASHER

"Why haven't you contacted Mr. Pendleton at the club yet?"

I learned a long time ago that there were no greetings or friendly phrases in my household. Once upon a time there might have been, but they vanished the same day my mother did.

Plucking a pear from the bowl on the black marble kitchen counter, I glance at my father. "Because I have no interest in working on his campaign this summer."

A heavy sigh rumbles from his throat. "Boy, do not make me remind you what happens when you don't follow orders."

It's a threat, one that I know is not empty, but I disregard it all the same. When I was a child, my father struck fear in my heart and mind. But these days, as I size him up, I realize that he's just an empty, hollow shell of a man.

Once a virulent, powerful man, David Frederick had been the most powerful kingmaker in all of London. He knew how to swoon and stomp, charming his way through ballrooms and back-alleys alike. To most people, he was still that almighty creator that placed unknowns into Parliament and could take down any opponent in one fell swoop. But to me, he was half the person he'd once been, toppled by the loss and betrayal of my mother.

"Fine, I'll contact him. But it's worthless work anyway, Oxford will still be waiting." He follows me as I traipse around our Downing Street brownstone, through the opulent rooms and up the sleek hardwood staircase.

"Don't walk away from me while I'm talking to you!" He was getting a taste for just how hard it was to control me these days.

"You made me into this, Father. I'm my own man, taking no orders from anyone. Aren't you proud?" I sneer, turning to face him.

I'd grown up in a house devoid of love or adoration, and I guess for the English, that was sometimes par for the course. I didn't weep for myself or dwell on it, but I did like to shove it in his face whenever I could. He'd created this monster, the one with the black soul and selfish, cocky attitude.

He ignores me. "How are you doing with the girl?"

A pang, so slight my heart doesn't even register it, vibrates through me. Is it grief, unease? I push it aside.

Father conceived the plan, from a young age I'd heard details and drunken rumblings, but when he'd learned of her arrival just months earlier, the idea had planted itself and he'd shared it with me. A way to finally bury Bennett McAlister six feet under.

"It's slow going, but I'm winning her over." I share because deep down, I want him to be proud of something I do. Even if it is deplorable.

"Good, good. You need to gain her trust. Seduce her, use whatever means necessary to get into her good graces. And then when the time is right, we'll strike."

There was so much malicious animosity in his green eyes that it was often difficult to catch a glimpse of the man who he used to be. Maybe after this was done, after the guillotine had fallen, maybe he would return to his former self. Perhaps that old shine, the playful sophisticate would come back. At least that's what I was hoping for. If I could do this for him, to bring him closure, I'd go to any lengths necessary.

"Tell me again why *I* must do this."

"Getting soft on me, chap?" My father chuckled, leading me into his study. On the mantel sat dozens of framed family photos, my smiling mother shining out from each.

I needed to hear it again, needed the fuel to keep moving forward.

He clasped his hands together as he stood looking at her pictures. "Bennett McAlister ruined our family. He took your mother, turned her into a heathen. He drove her to secrets and lies, and eventually her death. And then he acts like he doesn't even know us? Can't even acknowledge the hand he played in her downfall? A man, no a *boy*, like that doesn't deserve to be king. We must reveal who he truly is, we must avenge your mother's death."

As my father talks, the fury inside my bones pulses, all the way down to the marrow. His words fuel the demons that have haunted me, haunted this house, since she passed. And I realize, I'm not just doing this for him.

I grew up without a mother, I remember the horrific pictures the media printed after her death. Of the car being pulled from the river, of the twisted, mangled side of the bridge where she veered off.

It was time to get some closure, for both of us. Even if it meant sinking to the bottom, never resurfacing from the river of grief that was always nipping at my heels.

Boats cut through the water like seamless torpedoes gliding over the surface of the Thames.

The men in them move in sync, resembling machines rather than humans. If a rowing team is the real deal, if they're *that* ace, it doesn't even take effort to out maneuver another boat. They simply work, unthinking and unfeeling.

That is how I hope my team operates today, like cogs in a well-oiled machine.

Turning back to the pre-regatta festivity, Ed is downing drinks in front of my face.

"All the Lagavulin a bloke could want." He makes a refreshed noise as he sips the last dregs.

"Some of us are actually competing today." I actually like having him here, though, for he distracts me from the race.

"And some of us are here for the free alcohol and pretty birds. Look at them in their floral regatta dresses. Damn, I love a good race day."

He motions across the room, where a bunch of attractive girls in white and pink frocks stand chatting together. Ed's right, of course, it is always uplifting to have something nice to look at before I row.

My eyes must linger too long, because before I know what's happening, he's snapping his fingers in my face.

"Mate, she's not there."

Annoyed, I pretend to pick non-existent fuzz off of my warm-up kit. "What?"

"The question you should pretend to ask is 'who?' And you know who you're looking for. Nora Randolph, the family hasn't arrived yet. Hey, did you really humiliate her in Advanced Math the other day? Classic way *not* to get the girl, chap."

Ed is shaking his head as I think about the quiz in class last week. Who the hell knew that Nora was a genius? A full-fledged one too, as clearly she didn't want anyone to know. She'd hid it, taking her hand down even though she'd done brilliantly on that horrific pop quiz Mullins had given. Why did she care if people knew she was smart? Clearly, she was more than your average brainiac, but who gave a piss about that?

"I know what I'm doing." I wink at him, knowing he has no clue about my plan. "Girls like that love when you make them feel small, it gives her a chance to show me how tough she is. Gets her fired up, it's like foreplay in a way. Outing her little Mensa moment just gives her another reason to push back at me. Don't worry, she'll come around."

My friend laughs as he starts on another glass of whisky. "You're a bloody wanker, but I love you."

"Cheer for me, yeah?" I slap him on the back and don't wait for an answer. I don't need his luck, but I need to get down to the river.

As I walk through the doors and out into the garden that borders the Thames River House, a rare London sun peeks out between the clouds. The flowers and shrubbery are boasting in the rays, and I can smell the mist coming off of the water. I feel it in my bones, we're going to win this regatta.

"Oh, excuse me, young man."

A tall man walks past me as I step aside, the sun glinting in my eyes. As I turn, five people follow him. One of them being an elegantly dressed Nora, who is trying very hard to ignore me.

And that man? Bennett Fucking McAlister himself.

"Nora, nice to see you came to cheer me on." I tip my head, the group turning around toward me.

Anger roils in my gut, simmering like poison around my veins. Of course he doesn't recognize me, the arrogant prat. His smile, a polite and genuine grin, makes me want to rip his goddamn heart out.

"Oh, Nora, I didn't realize you had a friend in the regatta?" Bennett beams down at her, his obvious adoration for his soon-to-be stepdaughter shining for everyone to see.

Nora's face is half-hidden by a sunhat, the floral dress she wears clinging to her in all of the right places. How badly I want to unwrap the material from around her, get my fingers all over that skin. Every time I'm near her, my fingers seem to twitch with the need to move toward her body.

Nora inclines her head, those red tendrils glistening in the sun. "Well, I wouldn't necessarily call Asher and I friends, but it doesn't mean I can't have a good time watching my first rowing race."

The tall, redheaded woman standing next to her, her mother, I recognize from the papers, nudges her a bit. What she said was rude, especially at a regal event such as this.

"I'm sure my stepdaughter means no such thing, good luck today!" Bennett chuckles and whispers something in Nora's ear as they all walk off.

She doesn't look back at me, and it's probably best that she didn't. Or she would have seen how tightly my fists were clenched, the blunt nails digging half-moons into my palms.

Did I not look like her? With the same greens eyes and cheekbones. Could he not recognize the woman he betrayed and left for dead?

Adrenaline rocketed through my system, giving me even more fuel to kick some serious arse in the race. And Nora, she may not have known she was coming to watch me, but I knew that for the rest of the day I'd feel those hazel eyes on me.

Twenty minutes later and I'm sitting in my usual eight spot, commonly referred to as the stroke. Eye to eye with the coxswain, the seat is reserved for the most competitive, leader-driven person of the lot, and that has always been me. I set the pace, dictating to the rest of the boat how hard and fast I want them to be rowing. The position is only fit for the best, and once I'd started rowing as a child, I knew I would never let myself be anything but.

"You all ready to go?" Our coxswain, a rigid British twenty something named Peter who was as good as he was unhumorous.

We all nod in unison, and he starts his commands. My hands wrap around the oars, the polished wood firm against my clenched fists. I grip back, feeling my pulse thump steadily. Even in the toughest of races, I stayed cool as a cucumber. My adrenaline could be spiking, the need to win stronger than a ton of bricks on my back, and my pulse remained steady and normal.

"All four! Full slide!" he shouts at us, his commanding voice booming over the boat.

I don't bother to look at the other boats next to us, with the similar rowing teams in different colored uniforms. We are going to win, I don't need to intimidate or manipulate out here.

But as we get into position, my gaze slides over to the shore.

She's the target and my eyes are the heat-seeking missiles, they always seem to find Nora.

She's sitting on a chair right at the edge of the dock, where a bunch of the royals and nobles are seated. As if she can read my thoughts, an eyebrow perks, and I can see a hint of challenge beneath her hat. Next to her, Bennett sits smiling out at the water.

Rage and the dare that hangs between Nora and I swim inside my stomach, sparking and growing into something bigger. A monster, one that sits on my chest and pounds like a furious animal.

"Ready all ... row!" Peter whistles and we're off.

He barks commands at me, setting the pace, watching the others as they fall in line. I speed up, gaining momentum, my muscles already burning. I should slow down, conserve energy for the rest of the nearly four-minute race, but I can't. The unfamiliar look he gave me, the way she sat watching me from the dock, the pictures of my mother's car being dragged from the water ... it all mixes in my head like some kind of cruel movie.

We're miles ahead of the other boats, the water kicking up in front of us, streams of cold navy through the air. My legs burn with passion, my arms with competition.

I don't even realize when we're past the finish line until Peter is screaming at me in my face. "Way enough! Way enough!"

My brain snaps out of its fuzz as the guys cheer around me, raising their oars and hollering over the victory.

And to my surprise, when I finally let go of my death grip and reach down to my wrist, my pulse is hammering harder than it ever has in my life.

Taking a sip of tea, I listen on like a good little girl as the adults have their conversation.

"I just knew we should have planted geraniums instead of tulips in the back gardens, but Fernando would not listen to me." The wife of some Lord rambles on, boring us all to death about her gardener and his apparently "insane" tactics.

My mother, ever the social butterfly, can feel the conversation lacking. "I know I'm just the American, but have any of you watched that new show on Netflix? *The Great British Bake Off*?"

One of the other women holds her hand to her heart. "Oh, my dear, that isn't new! It's been on for *years*, but I must say I absolutely *adore* it."

"Ah, silly me, but I adore it as well! I just wish I could make all of those things, they look delicious." My mom takes a sip of her tea, setting it down in just the fashion that the etiquette coach brought in to help us taught her how to do.

"I'm always fascinated by how they make their custard just the right consistency, it looks so tasty."

I tune out as the women go on about the show, but at least it's better than gardening and plants.

A tap on my shoulder has me snapping back, my hat hitting something as I turn.

"Oh, sorry about that, love." A familiar voice fills my ears as my hat is put back the right way.

"Asher Frederick, what a pleasant surprise. You performed wonderfully today, bravo." One of the women fawns over him, and he puts on that chauvinistic grin that makes me want to slap him.

"Well, thank you, madam. It was my pleasure, a real rouser today."

"Nora, is this your friend?" Mom raises an eyebrow at me, and I know she's trying to telepathically let me know he's cute.

I try to telepathically tell her he's an asshole. "Mom, this is Asher Frederick, we go to Winston together."

He sticks out a hand, and then on second thought, bows a little. "Your highness, it's an honor."

Mom laughs, a real bellow. The other women look a little affronted, but they've become a little accustomed to her and they don't mind her.

"Oh, honey, you do not have to say that to me ... I'm not even really in the family yet. Mrs. Randolph, or better Rachel, will do just fine. That was a great race today."

"Thank you. Nora, would you like to take a walk with me?"

Mom gives me another look, and I swear if no one else could hear or see us, she would give me a fist bump and tell me to "go girl." I don't want to go anywhere with him, much less for a walk. That's some kind of innocent euphemism, and I don't feel like dealing with the devil today. Especially after what he did to me at school, exposing me like that.

But it would be rude to rebuff him here, and I don't want to give these busybodies any reason to discuss me further than they probably already do.

"Sure, I would like that."

I can practically hear the pants being charmed off of the women sitting around the table. I have to physically bite my tongue to keep from rolling my eyes.

Once we're far enough away from the group, I round on him. "What's this all about, Asher?"

Those green eyes grin, and I swear if he ever fully turned his efforts on, I'd be a goner. I was half-gone as it was.

"I want to show you something. And you look absolutely smashing today, might I add." His biceps flex in that rowing uniform, and instead of being gross, the smell of his sweat is so enticing my tongue actually darts out.

But I don't feel like playing his games. "No, you can't add that. What is it?"

Asher smiles again, and I hate, but also love, this teasing. "I like you when you're cheeky. Just follow me, alright?"

I shouldn't, because of all of the reasons he's given me not to thus far, but I can't help it. There is something so magnetizing about Asher; he has that perfect mix of English gentleman and British bad boy. In that rowing uniform, the tight shorts and shirt plastered to his body, I can see every muscle, every bulge. It has unwanted heat licking at my neck, and I want to yell at my traitorous body.

Asher leads me up a flight of stairs in the dockyard's big glass event space, where the after-regatta celebrations are being held. The space is all old wood and floor-to-ceiling windows, the glass sprayed with the mist from the Thames so close by. It smells like the river, and all of the furniture is comfortable and antique. To be honest, I'd like to come back here with a book and curl up beneath one of the windows overlooking the beautiful view.

Asher pushes open a door, and we walk into a room where pictures, plaques and trophies adorn every wall.

"This is one of my favorite places." He almost whispers it,

and I'm kind of shocked that he would tell me something that seems so personal.

"Because it's filled with medals and trophies?" There is an edge to my voice, a mocking sarcasm. I feel like a bitch, but I can't trust myself around him. Especially when he seems to be letting me in.

Looking at me, he shakes his head slightly and gives me a small smile. "No, although I do love winning. That's not why though. See, this room is steeped in history. We in England love our history, and the history of my sport is my favorite kind."

He walks slowly around the room, pointing out what are likely his favorite articles or memorabilia in here. Then to the window, which overlooks the Thames from an almost aerial view. The room is circular, almost as if we're at the top of a lighthouse.

"You can also see every facet of the water from up here, study it."

I'm looking at one of the photos, getting lost in his voice, when I feel a sizzling warmth at my back.

"I couldn't help but see you admiring my stroke out there."

Velvet, hot electricity fills me from head to toe, and I'm scared to turn around. To see the expression those eyes hold. He was this close to me once before, in the club in Paris. I'd stopped it then, blaming it on the music and alcohol.

But here, I have nowhere to hide. Asher is so close I can practically taste the mist on his body, smell the autumn water in his ink black hair.

"That's my position, you know. The stroke. I command the motion of the boat, make sure everyone falls in line and picks up on my rhythm."

I flush a hot pink under the collar, his conversation so dirty and thinly veiled that I think I hear myself start to pant.

"I saw that challenge in your eyes, by the way. And I'm here to collect my prize."

Hands, rough and weathered from the wood of the oars, gently circle my waist. I can't help the tremble that starts from the balls of my feet and sweeps over my skin, an audible groan escaping my lips. I know what is coming, what he's going to do. I don't want it.

But I do. I want it so badly that I've never wanted anything so desperately before. This is a feeling I've read about in books, the moment when the need to connect physically with another person is so strong that your brain snaps off and nothing but your heart fuels every decision. I never believed in the theory, feeling with your heart instead of thinking with your brain. It's too emotional, and science was a proven fact, something tangible that I could memorize and repeat over and over again in the same way.

Slowly I turn, Asher coming into view. He's bristling with arousal, the electricity of it buzzing all over his skin. Those green eyes are so dark, like the forest after a thunder storm. They're filled with a mixture of desire and hatred, and I know that they mirror my own. His jaw tics, like he's been holding back the urge to kiss me ever since we met.

Backing me up against the wall, his eyes never leave mine and his fingers dig into the material of my dress.

And then he does.

Tilts his head, drags his tongue across his bottom lip, smirks the slightest bit, and covers my mouth with his.

The shock hits me first, coursing through my bones while they seize up and my heart gallops at a champion filly's pace. I've never had another person's lips touch my own, aside from my mothers. Never a boy, one with a man's build.

Never in my wildest dreams would I have imagined that the

boy who torments and entices me would be the one to grant me my first kiss.

Asher's mouth pries at my unmoving lips, his warm, wet taste sending fireballs of lust rocketing between my thighs. When I don't respond, he increases the pressure, trapping my head between his rough hands and delving deeper into the kiss.

That sets me off, the hunger he's feeding me from his own body. My lips move, tentatively at first. But then my whole body gets involved, the storm of fire picking up like brush catching the wind. His skill gives me the education I need, his body meeting every curve of my own and pressing in all of the right places.

A moan rumbles through my throat and past his lips, and an answering growl vibrates past my tongue, lighting me up from the inside out. He's stealing my breath, making it hard to breath between his deep and exploring taste of my mouth. He keeps his hands on my hips, even though I want them to move up and down my body. Besides his hands and lips keeping my locked into place, no other points of connection are being made between us. In a deep part of my brain, the part that isn't dazing out on the drug of his kiss, I find it odd that he isn't pressing this further.

Had I challenged him to this? Had I known that all along we would end up here? I would be lying to myself if I said that I hadn't.

"Stroke. That's why I'm so good at it." His accent is dark and stormy as he pulls away.

I'm not sure what he looks like at this moment, because I can't seem to open my eyes. I just feel for the wall, hoping it will hold me up as my knees knock together.

Asher's breath hits my ear. "I'll see you around, princess."

And then his hands are gone, the raw scent of male leaves

the room. After several seconds of focusing on nothing but gulping air in and blowing it out, I open my eyes.

I run on facts and logic. Theories and conclusions.

But what just happened in this room defies all of that, leaving me feeling as if I've never *truly* known anything in my entire life.

A ssuming the natural progression of life, I always thought that my mother would be the one helping me plan a wedding someday.

But with her high-profile engagement and laissez-faire attitude about the grand event that would be her nuptials, I found myself pushing her along to pick out the noteworthy details. And some not-so-noteworthy details.

"Honestly, sweetheart, I could marry Bennett in the back garden of this place and call it a day. Just two rings, an ordained person, and I'd be happy as a clam. I already am. I don't understand why everyone is interested in what thousand-dollar designer gown I'm going to wear."

Mom slumps into her hands, samples of taffeta and napkin colors piling up over her head.

This is how she's been about the entire wedding ever since the paparazzi attacked her viciously the first time we set foot on European soil. She simply followed the man she loved, and was being harassed and judged at every turn. I knew I was too, but Mom was bearing the brunt of it and I felt sad for her. It was supposed to be one of the happiest times of her life, and she was all but canceling the whole big shebang.

I had always been the one out of both of us who organized life in general. She made the real money and all of the property was in her name, but I paid the bills. I had a schedule set up for auto-withdrawals and direct deposits. When the cable or Internet went out, I called the company. If the electricity bill seemed too high, I was the one who argued with the idiots on the phone until they gave us a credit. I made the dentist appointments, I monitored when the car needed an oil change. Not that my mother wasn't an adult, she was a fully capable woman who supported us. But I was also a part of the family, and I wanted to contribute in the way my brain best allowed me. Honestly, I enjoyed keeping the books, so to speak.

"Because you're their fairy tale, Mom. You are the woman every little girl wants to be, getting swept off of her feet by the handsome prince." I do a little flourish with my hands.

She looks up, tears threatening. I know how stressful this has been on her.

"Come on, look. You're getting an all-expenses paid day to live out your wildest dreams. The world's biggest names when it comes to catering, dresses, shoes, makeup ... they all want to be a part of it. I know it's tedious and every decision you make is scrutinized, but come on. Who cares what those people think?! You get to pick whatever you want, go as extravagant as you please. And then, at the end of the day, it will still be about two people who fell in love. So let's do this, have fun with it!"

I put an extra sparkle in my smile to get her mood up. Finally, she sits up straight, some of that Randolph confidence filling out her slim form.

"Okay, you're right. Gosh, how did I raise such an awesome kid?"

"It was all you, Mom. But I must say, I'm pretty fab." I shrug like I just can't help it.

She reaches over and puts her arm around my shoulder. "We are blessed, and I need to stop complaining about the gifts we've been handed because some people are arseholes."

Her use of the British phrase makes me crack up, because she's been working on her accent which is terrible.

"Yes, we are, now which color do you want these linens to be?"

We go through samples of everything from linens to dress fabric to flower colors and arrangements for the next half an hour. Mom actually seems excited about some of the choices, one of which includes a mini-Philly cheesesteak as an appetizer for the cocktail hour. We insisted on having some of our own culture and traditions included, and Bennett was nothing but supportive.

"So, how about the guest list?" Mom looks up as I'm scrolling through my phone looking at the options for tiaras that the royal jeweler sent to my email.

"What about it?" I'm distracted, so I don't see or hear the hint in her expression.

"Did they give you a plus one?"

This makes me put my phone down. "Why would they give me a plus one? I'm going to be running around like crazy just keeping you calm and happy."

Mom frowns. "It's a day for you to enjoy and celebrate in as well, and if you really need to be doing those things for me, then it won't be a good day. Plus, it looks like you might have a ... friend that you'd like to celebrate the day with."

Her expression is all coy and sneaky, and my apprehension rises. I don't like where this is going at all. "Um, I barely have any friends here."

"That's not what it looked like at the regatta." She sips her tea, her eyes sparking with curiosity.

I roll my eyes, staring down at my own tea. One of the wait-staff brought it in, something they did every afternoon regard-less of whether we asked for it or not. I was actually starting to get used to it, and the act of afternoon tea was calming.

Except for right now. "Asher and I are not friends, Mom. I just ... know him from class."

She makes a sound that says she's not convinced. "That was not a boy who looked like he was just 'in your class.' He's inter-ested in you, honey. And he's cute, like really cute. That makes me a cougar or something, but I say it in the most non-weird way possible. Maybe it's time that you let yourself have a little fun. I also sound like the worst parent in the world suggesting that, but you live your life more responsibly than most forty year olds I know. You need to go a little crazy."

I can't help but snort out a laugh. "Who would have thought this would ever be a normal mother-daughter conversation that we would have?"

But her words do hit me in a part of my heart that feels so unexplored, it is basically another planet. For the thousandth time since I've moved here and started at Winston, I question why I haven't ventured outside of my safe little intellectual bubble.

Mom leans over, taking a hold of my hand. "We are not the normal kind of people. Look at us."

She points to the ballroom we sit in, the one placed right in the middle of Kensington Palace. You know, the place that we live.

"Maybe you're right ... but I'm not saying yes to a plus one."

Mom puts on her singsong voice. "But you're thinking about it!"

She was right. I was thinking about it.

G etting to someone's weak spot, or exploiting their inner most need, has become an art form for me.

I'm exceedingly good at reading people, at knowing their motivations and personality within the first five minutes of meeting. It's like a gift and a curse; I can instantly tell which kind of people I will like, or at least respect, and which will drive me bloody mad until the day I can get away from them.

One of the things that drives me absolutely bonkers is that I *can't* get a read on Nora Randolph. My first mistake was assuming that she was the typical brat who comes into fame and fortune. As I've found out, she could care less about the money. In school, on the trip to Paris, any of the other times I've interacted with her ... she's not once talked about expensive shoes or jewelry or trips to far off places. Nora had only wanted to see the Eiffel tower, or watch the boat race, or study.

The second mistake I made was in letting her convince me that was all she was. Because I may be a good liar, but Nora was a decent one too. She masked her real personality, hid her intellect and her opinions. Her anger was always thickly veiled, and any mention of her former life is nonexistent.

I'd gotten cocky in my haste to take down her stepfather, but I needed to do more recon.

Which was exactly why I'd semi-stalked Nora on the way home from school today. I'd noticed a while ago that she'd begun ducking her security detail and walking home through the park by Winston Academy. Which just so happened to back right up to Regent Street, the main shopping district in London.

"Hi, princess." I stroll up next to her, making sure to turn on my extra-charm smile.

At first, she tries to ignore that I'm even there, but that familiar electricity crackles between us. That's fine, I like the challenge. And now that I've misjudged her, I want even more to expose her soft spot.

Something feels different, though. Typically, the girls I pursue play hard to get as an act, and I know the whole time that I am the one in control. But after that kiss ... bloody Christ could that girl kiss ... I felt a little ... off my game. She seemed to have some knowledge over me now, and maybe I'd gone too far with the kiss after the race. It was making me second guess all of my moves, and I silently cursed myself for letting a girl like Nora get in my head.

"Don't you have anything better to do than follow me around all day like a lovesick puppy?"

Her snarly tone went straight to my balls, and I knew I was sick and twisted for it but I didn't care.

"Actually, love, I don't. You're the most interesting thing in all of London, or didn't you know?

"Coming from the self-proclaimed con-artist of the foggy city, I guess I should take that as a compliment." Her tongue burns almost as hot as the color of her hair.

And it's as if she sees right through me. But Nora could never guess my real motives for growing close to her.

"Exactly. So how about it, let's go on a date." I catch a strand of her hair in the wind, the silky lock slipping through my fingers.

She yanks away. "Don't you know anything about personal boundaries? And no, I am not going on a date with you."

We head onto the busy street, one packed with tourists and Londoners alike, popping in and out of the trendy shops lining the pavement.

"Okay, I get it. I'm good enough to snog, but not good enough to date." The corner of my mouth flicks up at the memory of pinning her against the wall in the boathouse.

Nora stops as if someone has completely yanked her chain, and then gets real close, waving a finger in my face. "Let's get one thing straight. You are the one who has pursued me. You are the one who kissed me. I've wanted none of it. And what the hell is wrong with you anyway? The first day of school, you basically threatened me. And now you're trying to date me? You're psychotic."

I'd been called worse. "Maybe we should kiss and make up then?"

Nora throws up her hands and stomps away. "You drive me batshit crazy!"

Increasing my pace to catch up with her, I chuckle. "Maybe that's what you're looking for in a lad. How about this? Hang out with me this afternoon, and if you don't thoroughly enjoy yourself, I'll leave you alone."

My words dangle between us, the honk of cabs and whoosh of red double deckers around us the only sounds that register. My idea is just crazy enough to work, but if she accepts, I need to pull out all of the stops to hook her for good.

Those hazel eyes seem to work around the idea, and I can

practically hear the cogs in her brain digesting it. That brain, God I would love to learn more about that.

"Fine. But this is it. After today, you take a hike." She crosses her arms over her chest, and my eyes flit to the small opening in her uniform blouse.

"Don't be so sure about that. But, it's a deal that I'm willing to take. Come on then, we're almost there."

I walk ahead, waiting to hear her black chunky school shoes behind me. I skirt tourists and look for my destination, knowing it is the one place that she'll be vulnerable with me. If I'm going to succeed in pulling her closer to me, then I can't take her to a fancy restaurant. She would never sit somewhere like a coffee shop and chat about the nonsense of our lives. No, we need fun. Interaction. And judging from that kiss, as hot as bollocks as it was, Nora is naïve. Inexperienced.

"This is where you really want to go?" She peers up at the sign of the store I'm stopped in front of.

"You're not a proper Londoner until you've bought your first toy from Hamley's. So, this is where we are going."

A toy store is the perfect place to arse off, and if this can't get Nora to loosen up around me, I'm not sure what will. And although she still has a sourpuss expression on her face, I can see the childlike interest in her eyes. Finally, I'm making some inroads to figuring this bird out.

We enter the store, the staff smiling and welcoming us. I used to come here all the time as a boy, but haven't stepped foot in a toy store since I turned thirteen and a girl's baps were the most interesting toys I wanted to get my hands on.

Seven stories of wonder and awe, starting with the ground floor of every stuffed animal you could possibly think up. I know that further up, there is a floor worth of Harry Potter merchandise, and a Lego floor that even sparks my interest.

"Pick anything you'd like, it's on me." I have to laugh a little at her face.

Nora looks like she just walked into Christmas morning itself. She's probably too overwhelmed to be cheeky right now, because she just ignores me and begins to walk around.

Meandering through the shelves, she stops and picks up a pink spotted stuffed hippo. "I used to have one just like this."

I catch the look of homesickness that winks around the corner of her eyes, and the arsehole inside of me feeds on that insecurity.

"It must have been tough leaving the States ..." I want her to open up to me, even if it is for my own ill gains.

"Yes, sort of. But I love my mom, so it wasn't so hard." Not the soul-professing answer I was looking for, but at least she isn't biting my head off.

As we walk, I study her body and movement. She's long but lean, like an elegant gazelle. Nora moves almost silently around the store, and if she were any other person, the customers in the store would be all over her. I'm surprised that no one has recognized her yet, but she sinks into the racks and blends so that barely anyone notices her. I find it fascinating yet alarming, how a girl this beautiful can go unseen; takes skill and practice. Those long legs under the uniform plaid skirt, skin I just want to run my hands over and watch blush with desire.

Wordlessly, she moves to the escalator and I follow, not having gotten anything out of her but the one sentence.

"What was your favorite board game growing up? I was a Monopoly man myself, you know snatching up property and money has always been my thing." I wink at her as the escalator goes up.

Those peach lips tip up. "You would. No, I was more of a Clue girl. Figuring out the mystery, using logic. And I have always loved a good thriller."

"Ah, okay. So you fancied Nancy Drew then?"

Nora scoffs. "Try Agatha Christie."

"Are you the type of person who reads the last chapter and spoils the book?" Now we're getting somewhere.

"Of course not, that's cheating. But really, what was the last book you even read?" She walks onto the second floor and almost steps on the large train set lining the floor.

I catch her elbow, the feel of her beneath my fingers like silk and something forbidden.

"Oops, thank you." She looks sheepish but I know that I'm slowly making her warm up to me.

"And for your information, I am a big Dan Brown fan. So don't think I'm some big tosser." I fold my arms over my chest, and I notice when her eyes shoot down to study my pecs through my uniform button up.

"Funny, I thought it would be something stereotypical like Winston Churchill's war journals or something along those lines." Nora picks up a cool looking stamp set and places it back down.

"But Clue, yeah? That film used to scare the bollocks out of me. The one with that wonky butler character."

Nora laughs as we head for the third floor. "Me too, actually. But I was always Professor Plum."

"Not Miss Scarlett?" My eyes heat as I obviously look her over.

She actually makes contact and hits my arm slightly. "Brains always ruled over looks in my corner of the world, Frederick."

Tilting my head, sincerity pops out of my mouth before I can come up with a plotted phrase. "I think I like you more for that fact."

Nora's eyes hold something akin to shock and endearment, and I'm speechless for one of the only times in my life. Because it's true, I do kind of like her for all of the things that make her different from other girls.

The third floor looks like pink and flowers lost its stomach all over the walls. Baby dolls, cartoon makeup, Barbie's, Cabbage Patch Kids and every imaginable girl toy that could ever be shoved into a dollhouse resided on this floor.

"Oh God, let's get out of here please." Nora heads right for the up escalator, and I'm surprised once more.

"What, the princess doesn't like princesses?"

Her amber eyes flash. "According to you, I'm a peasant, not a princess. And no, I never was one for all of the flash and makeup."

She threw my words of our first meeting right back at me. "About that, I may have made a small clanger."

I follow the long waves of red off the moving stairs and onto the fourth floor, one with a random assortment of toys.

"A clanger?" Nora looks confused.

"A mistake, a misjudgment. I thought you knew everything, girl genius."

A blush tinges her high cheekbones. "You forget that we have different slang where I come from. If I asked you what jawn, youse, or jimmies were, you wouldn't know, now would you?"

Chuckling, she's got me. "I suppose not."

Something must catch her eye, because she doesn't bother to answer me.

But at least this is going better than I thought it was. She may think she's only giving me trivial information, but some of these likes and dislikes give me insight into her personality. Nora likes to read mysteries and thrillers, which means that she is attracted to complications and puzzles. Frilly, fancy things don't hold her interest, and she's smart as a whip. And through our meandering talk, I've picked up on all of her body language. The way her cheeks pink when I say something that makes her blood warm. How her eyes slant to the right when she's trying to be cheeky, but I know she secretly likes to sass me. Every time she is in the vicinity of another person, she all but vanishes, skirting around them and trying to go as unnoticed as possible.

All of these little clues, little quirks, will help me get closer to her. Help me insert myself into her life. And when I have her good and wrapped around my finger, I'll get closer to crushing the one person who has made my life a living hell.

"This is what I want." Nora interrupts my thoughts as she holds up a box that is almost as big as she is.

"That's really what you want?" My face must be one of disapproving confusion.

"You said whatever I want, and this was your idea in the first place. So carry this down and grant my wish."

I can't help but take the innuendo she's given me. "Oh, love, I'll grant any wish you desire."

Again, her cheeks go scarlet with embarrassed arousal.

But, I take the large chemistry set box from her hands and lug it down the escalators, out to the cash registers and pay for the thing. When I'd decided to take her here, it was the last thing I'd ever guess she would buy. Then again, it was why I'd done it, to try and anticipate more about her personality and actions.

As we parted on the sidewalk and I put her in a taxi, I didn't even try to kiss her. I pretended to be the perfect gentleman, putting the large box in the back and opening her door. Then I'd winked and she'd smiled and waved as the car drove off.

I'd mark the day overall as a win in my book. But as I grabbed my own taxi home, I couldn't help but feel a mixed sea of emotions swirling about in my stomach. I was closer to my end goal, but I realized as the car turned onto Downing Street, that I was actually coming to like Nora Randolph.

And that was the last thing I needed.

I'd gone soft as a hardboiled egg.

For the first time in eighteen years, I'd let someone my own age, of the opposite sex, break through my tough outer shell. And I was just as surprised as anyone that it was Asher Frederick.

But after the toy store, he'd finally worn me down enough to the point that I was letting him be seen with me in the hallways at Windsor. And walk me home after school.

And kiss me up against the stone security walls surrounding Kensington Palace, the parts where no guards would see us.

In the weeks since our impromptu hangout, Asher had managed to erase my initial thoughts about him. Okay, not erased. Because I was a teenage girl and I still went back to that first day in the hall, and the trip to Paris, and his intimidating nature. But at the toy store, he had been like a different person. An open, honest and friendly boy ... one who talked about books and wanted to get to know me. One who joked about stuffed animals and what outfits were sexiest on Barbie's. Which Harry Potter character he'd liked best growing up; Ron, surprisingly.

And each day Asher revealed a new, better side of himself. On one walk home, he'd introduced me to Radiohead as we walked along sharing his earbuds. I'd actually flirted and been bold enough to reach out and grasp his hand since we'd been walking so closely together. At a coffee shop last week, he'd ordered me a chocolate croissant as I picked a table in the back. And he'd known to do that because I'd brought one for breakfast just two days earlier.

I was finding that for the first time, it was nice to be noticed. Usually I tried to fade into the background, but with the attention Asher gave me, I felt like stepping into the sunlight. We hadn't really done much of it in public—most of our interaction had been one-on-one or walking together but not touching at school—and I had started to think that maybe he didn't want people to know about our ... I didn't even know what to call it.

God, I was so becoming the kind of girl I used to loathe. Who cared what he wanted or if he had the need to hide me or what we were doing? Also, why was I concerning myself with this?

Each time he texted me or smiled at me or met me somewhere to hang out, a tiny alarm bell sounded in my brain. *Remember what he said before you softened up to him.* And every time, I pushed it aside. London was turning me into a masochist. Maybe it was something in the water.

Maybe it was just Asher Frederick.

I didn't often watch romantic comedies or read romance novels, but the few I did always followed the same guidelines. Your life was perfectly average until the world put the ultimate wrecking ball in your way in the form of a man. The specific man designed for that specific woman, the one who would knock her knees out from under her and cause her to become a raving lunatic. But it was okay, because in the end they found love and the world was righted.

Was I becoming that lunatic? And did he feel the same way?

I shook my head to physically clear it as I walked through the front doors of Winston. And as I turned the corner, I spotted him. My stomach began to flutter with that nervous energy that only seemed to be honed by him. I took in every inch of Asher's long, lean body. From the dark mop of styled hair, to the strong jaw and jewel-like eyes, so green they looked like the lush trees of rainforests I'd read about in books. My gaze traveled down his form, the rower's muscles barely contained beneath the neat school uniform. And even though every other boy in school wore it, it looked like it had been tailor-made for Asher Frederick.

He was the definition of a school girl crush. The boy that every girl had thought about when she listened to love songs in her bedroom and wrote in her diary. But he also had that bad boy lurking beneath the skin, the one you wanted to sneak out with and hide from your mother.

I had never been the girl who'd attracted the attention from someone the likes of him, but miraculously, his eyes seemed to be glued to me as well.

And so did his lips. My core flushed just from the thought of those lazy, dragging kisses he left me with at the end of our walks home. Asher hadn't caught on yet that I was a virgin. And when I say virgin, I mean to everything. He was the first boy I had ever kissed.

His eyes catch me staring, and he raises an eyebrow in greeting. I make it to my locker before I realize he is there beside me, leaning his back against the polished wood and looking all kinds of delicious.

"And how are you today, love?" He doesn't touch me, but I can feel the heat passing between us.

I pretend not to sneak a glance at him as I pull out a book

from my locker. "Oh you know, same old. There is some popular kid trying to get my attention."

"Is that so? In that case, I'll have to bloody kill him." He turns so that his massive shoulder leans against the lockers.

Over the past month, I've become obsessed with Asher's arms. They're naturally long, almost freakishly so, but all of the rowing has practically turned them into weapons. I want to hang off of them like my own personal jungle gym.

"Well, it's not like I'm seeing anyone, so I thought I'd give him a call." I know he loves it when I'm cheeky, and with Asher, I've somehow become versed in the art of flirting.

Those green eyes go onyx. "We'll just see about that."

He doesn't kiss me on the cheek as he walks away, but I feel the need to reach up and fan my face.

"I heard she polished his knob in the music room closet." A few giggles come from across the hall as I see three pairs of eyes dart away.

Huh?

"Are you dating Asher Frederick?"

Before I can even wrap my head around the rumor that just flew across the space between the lockers, I'm confronted by a tall blond girl standing in the space Asher just occupied.

"Um, I don't believe that is any of your business." I can't believe the defensive tone is coming from my mouth.

She leans over to the girls next to her. "I told you they were just shagging. Thanks!"

Her words and their malicious smiles feel like a full on slap in the face, and I haven't picked my jaw up off the floor even when they round the corner out of sight.

Is that what the other kids at Winston truly think? That I'm classless enough to be hooking up with someone I've known for barely three months? Not that it's classless, but I don't know.

They don't even know me. No one here knows I'm a virgin, and yet they're gossiping about my sex life like it's some big party and everyone is invited?

"Oh, darling, don't even let those silly slags get you down." Eloise came up to my locker, only a tiny Chanel purse slung over her shoulders.

In fact, I don't think I've ever seen her or another girl in this school carrying actual books. What the hell was I doing wrong?

"I ... uh, is that what everyone around here thinks?" I shuffle my feet as I sling my book laden bag around a shoulder.

She shrugs. "I mean, it is Asher, and this is high school. Albeit a very expensive, exclusive one. But the same things still go on here. Sex, drugs and rock and roll. But don't worry, even if you are knocking knickers, I won't spread it around."

"Oh, well thanks." I roll my eyes. "We aren't, by the way."

I don't ask about the "it is Asher" comment, because I'm too afraid to delve into the history surrounding him that I'm sure is filled with dirt and ex-flings.

"I'm all for whatever you want to do with your naughty bits, I encourage it." She holds her hands up.

"Eloise, seriously. We're not having sex. I'm not even with him."

She death glares me. "Well, I said you didn't have to tell me. But don't *lie* to me, love."

I huff. "This is insane."

"You're the one who decided to get caught in Asher's web." She walks next to me as I make my way to the next period.

"You're implying that he isn't the one infatuated with me. Why couldn't it be the other way around?"

At this, Eloise laughs. "Oh, darling, don't make me hiccup. You're about as innocent as a church mouse, and he's the Hugh Grant of Downing Street."

She clacks along in her non-approved black stilettos as I enter the door to my next class.

Her words stay with me throughout the period though. Maybe there is a lot I still need to learn about Asher. And maybe I've been jumping way ahead of myself after all.

17

Being among the elite families and notable persons of Europe, not to mention the world, came with its duties. My father, and by extension me, had a packed social calendar filled with parties, ceremonies, openings and charitable events.

While he attended one of these many boring functions almost every night, I was brought along to the most important ones as a way to show unity and bravado. He would walk me around like his pet, introducing me to new faces and schmoozing with old ones. I would one day be in his shoes, as he always reminded me.

Tonight was no different. The opening of a brand-new opera at the Vienna State Opera, and everyone who was anyone in our circle was there.

"I want to see you take another shot of Pimm's." Speri claps her hands behind me.

Our merry band of teenagers has already commandeered a balcony away from the arse-kissing and politics going on in the main lobby. It's like the Roman Colosseum down there, everyone is chummy until they're forced to rip out each other's throats.

The chandeliers glint off of the velvet seats and cascading murals, everything about the opera over-the-top and opulent. Women in their ball gowns and men in their three-piece tuxedos, some sporting canes or pocket watches. It was all for show, pomp and circumstance the one thing that got you further in our world than any other attribute. Sure, wit and cunning counted for something, but what was that saying? Fake it 'til you make it? That was how half the people in this room had scored an invitation to this event.

I take my hands off of the balcony railing where I'm observing the crowd below and instead turn my gaze to my friends.

Drake and Ed are sprawled in red velvet chairs, nursing four fingers of scotch each. Two familiar faces to our crowd, but ones that usually don't come out to these events, are Lillian and Alexander. Twin third years at Winston, their mother was the Secretary of State for Education and a big player in the world of the wealthy and powerful. They're goofing around, daring each other to do childish things and generally acting like tossers. Speri is almost a bottle down, which she hides well. And Katherine, Eloise and Nora sit on a large chaise lounge, chatting.

And Nora, my girl, she was legless. A laugh bubbled out of her mouth, and her eyes were sleepy with alcohol. I hadn't really been keeping track of how much she had to drink, as I needed to keep my eyes off of her.

If I looked straight at her, it would be like burning my retinas in the sun. Why she'd picked a dress the exact same color of the crushed red velvet the opera house sported was beyond me. Radiant. Breathtaking. Cock pummeling. I'd been sporting a stiffy all night, and each time I saw that fire-engine material stick to another desirable curve of her body, I had to bite my tongue in frustration.

"Ugh, it tastes like poison, I don't know how you all drink this stuff." She leaned back on the chaise, her breasts pushing up at the top of the strapless dress.

"It gets easier as you drink more. See?" Katherine downs another capful of the citrusy gin.

I don't know what made Nora let loose tonight. Maybe since she'd been to a couple of events and hung out with us, she felt more comfortable. She shouldn't, people like us weren't ones to trust, but she was naïve and gullible. Maybe she thought we were more of a ... thing, and that was making her feel like one of the group.

Regardless, she was drunk. And was playing right into my hands.

"Have another." I wink at her for extra encouragement.

"Okay, fine." She whistles a bit and downs another shot, and I can see it burn as she makes a sour face.

I will say, it's rather brilliant having her around to play with these days. Sure, I may be pretending to be a gentleman— walking her home from school and escorting her through the halls, hanging out in coffee shops and buying her favorite snacks —but it was all for show. Underneath, I was trying little ways to have the paparazzi find her. They'd caught us at a hookah bar on Edgeware Road, and crashed our date to Speaker's Corner in Hyde Park. Each time, I'd been sure to be holding her hand, or putting us out there in a certain way.

Slowly but surely I was trying to get to Bennett McAlister. Ruin his reputation. Slash his chances of becoming an integral part of the government or ascending the throne. Bury his perfect little life six feet under.

And getting the perks of snogging Nora and trying to get in her pants ... well those were just bloody bonuses.

Drake motions to Katherine, and they leave the secluded balcony. I guess I've known for a while now that they're shagging, but they're also shagging everyone else so it's not a big thing. There are only a few couples at Winston who are actually faithful to each other, and our gang would never be caught dead hanging around with those goody-two-shoes.

"Maybe we could go somewhere too."

A small, warm hand grips my bicep where it rests on the railing, and I move closer to Nora. She's drunk and randy, and here is yet another perk of having her as part of my plan. I turn to gather her in my arms, the need to feel her close becoming an intrinsic action these days.

For all of the scheming and naughtiness I've been indulging in, there is a small part of my conscience that kicks me in the bollocks and whispers in my ear. In the only light part of my soul still left, in the innocent, untainted corner, I could actually fancy Nora. In a real, genuine way. Sometimes, when we're alone, I don't have to pretend to be nice. It just comes naturally with her, and our banter flows and the way I'm attracted to her just feels ... normal.

But then the dark side bites back. I'm not fucking normal, and neither is she.

"Where do you want to go?" My nose is buried in her hair as I say it, my lips making contact with the sensitive part of her ear before she can answer.

She's warm and pliable in her knackered state, and even though I've had the equivalent of one beer, I'm not a good enough chap to stop.

"Take me somewhere." Her sigh is all I need to pull her toward the door of the balcony.

Up, up, up we go, through stairwells and hallways, all the while pausing to make out in dark corners until one of us breaks it off in search of privacy. There is something addicting about

Nora; the way her hair smells, the way her tongue dances with mine. I'm no stranger to a fit girl, but her innocence and will to learn from my body is exciting and arousing.

When I can no longer hear the chatter of the party below, I push open a heavy oak door and lock us in as it closes. It's some kind of sitting room, it must be used as a dressing room sometimes but tonight it's not occupied.

"Are you going to let me under that dress, pretty girl?" I walk her backwards until her back meets the white wall.

So far, it had just been a lot of hot and heavy snogging. Each time I tried to loosen a button on that private school uniform, she clammed up like a Scotland Yard-grade lock that I didn't have the combination to.

Nora giggles, but her eyes are molten. "I don't know ..."

I don't give her time to overthink it, but instead cover my mouth with hers. Slow and intoxicating, I set the pace. She may be drunk, but I'm in no rush. There is nothing else worth doing tonight, and I could spend the next four hours in here with her.

My hands grip her slim waist and move upward, my callouses catching on the smooth fabric of her dress. I can practically hear Nora purr as the tips of my fingers brush the sides of her breasts and move forward. Nothing is hindering my palms but the top of her dress, and even with it on I can feel the tightness of her nipples.

"Wait, Asher ..."

Bloody hell. I sigh, dropping my head on her shoulder because she is going to stop me from doing anything but getting very blue balls. *Again*. Managing to hide my annoyance and disappointment, I looked up into her eyes.

"I don't feel so well."

All of the desire and heat had vanished from her face, and left her skin pale and cold. Nora put her hands to her mouth and covered a gagging sound. Fuck all, she was sick, not prude.

And another boner bites the dust.

"Okay, let's sit down." An idea sprang into my head, one that would embarrass both she and her wanker of a stepfather. "Actually, why don't we go back downstairs, find your mother?"

If I was lucky, she'd toss her cookies in front of the entire opera house.

"Asher, Bennett is in an election season. If anyone sees me like this ... oh, God." She moans as she ducks her head between her legs again.

Oh I know it is, which is exactly why I'm here, interested in you.

"Don't worry, love. I'll take care of you."

I try to lift her, but her skin is cold and clammy, and she's falling about like a limp shoelace. I wasn't lying when I said she was legless before. The illness must have just overcome her, like it often can when drinking. I need to try to get her downstairs.

"I don't feel good." Her voice breaks on a cry, and a pang of guilt hits me.

"You're going to feel a bit wonky, love. Let's try to lie down."

Tonight isn't the night to do this. Or at least that's what I tell myself. After ten minutes of going on about it, Nora falls asleep, her thin, tall body curled up in a big arm chair in the corner of the room.

After she's zonked out, I can't convince myself to stay. It's bad enough I took pity on her at all, and I curse myself for that streak of softness inside me.

I slip out of the room and down the stairs, annoyed at how the night ended after so much promise.

"Asher." A sultry voice hits me as I round the corner.

Standing on the other side of the stairs in a heart-stopping black gown is Evelyn Stuttgart, the German heiress who has always been a trusted friend in times of need. Last year, we'd had a standing agreement to shag whenever it was convenient for each other. I don't know why it had waned, but sometimes we still saw each other at events.

And like tonight, I thought it might be brilliant to bring that agreement back.

"Evelyn, looking fit as always. How is Munich?"

She shrugs, her long black curls moving around her breasts as she stares at me, only one thing in those light blue eyes. She wanted to shag too, and after the annoyance with Nora, I was becoming very keen on the idea.

"Same old, you know I can never stay in one place for too long. Although I do miss our weekends in Monaco." The memories of our time spent on her father's yacht is some of my favorite wanking material.

"What brings you up here?"

"Nothing interesting on the ground floor. Although ... there could be something very interesting here."

Evelyn had never been the type to be vague or tentative. She crossed the space between us, her hands falling to my shoulders once she was in front of me. Her mouth came at mine, skilled but predictably practiced in its initial assault on my own.

And I let her. Ticked off at the predicament I was in, and wanting to do something reckless, it was as if the universe had sent Evelyn here to both tempt and seduce me.

She smelled like exotic flowers and expensive penthouses, and was womanly in a way that Nora was not. Evelyn was probably the fantasy girl of half the men in this place. And yet when she moved her lips down my neck, sucking and biting in the exact spots that would have had me stiff as a pole a year ago, nothing happens.

My knob is soft, a useless piece of anatomy in my trousers. Bloody hell, I can't stop thinking about a pair of blushing cheeks and hands that push mine away when I'm about to undress her.

Without words, I push her away from me and start down the stairs.

"What the hell, Asher?" I hear her raspy voice from behind me.

I don't bother answering. I'm too ashamed to, or too annoyed to.

Either way, my blood is boiling at the fact that I can't seem to get Nora, the girl I'm supposed to be toying with, out of my head.

18

NORA

Two days after the dreadful opera night, and my head and pride still felt like they'd taken a beating.

God, there were so many things to be embarrassed for. One, I'd never gotten so drunk in my life. In fact, before that night I had never truly been drunk.

I hadn't even properly gotten to see Vienna. Mom and Bennett had taken me on a short sightseeing tour the day after and I'd almost thrown up in the Schoenbrunn Tiergarten. By the time we visited St. Stephen's Cathedral, I had a migraine the size of Texas and Mom could see that I was struggling.

Instead of admitting all of the stupid things I'd done the night before, I lied and said it was an episode. It was the first time I'd ever lied so badly to my mother that a little piece of my soul broke off.

For the first time since my life had turned into a fairy tale, I seriously doubted my ability to handle this world of grandeur and power.

The flight back to London is miserable and rainy, with the November chill sending ice through my bones. Kensington

Palace looked dreary as the black town car containing myself, Mom and Bennett pulled up to its gates.

What should have been an adventurous mini-vacation, with sightseeing and some time spent with Asher, had gone down hill so quickly because of my stupid actions. I could have embarrassed myself, I could have given the tabloids more fodder. Worse, I could have ruined the event for Mom and Bennett, at a time so crucial for them that it might destroy everything they'd been working for.

But what I did find about the trip, or more what I didn't notice ... was the paparazzi. For the first time since we'd hopped the pond, I hadn't really been concerned with their shouts or accusations. I noticed myself moving into the buildings we were attending events at, letting their barbs slide off my skin as if it was slicked with oil. Was this what it was like to become fully immersed in the world of the elite? Was I becoming one of them?

And Asher. Oh God, I'd nearly thrown myself at him. If I hadn't gotten sick, would I have let him take me further than I'd ever been before? It sure had seemed like it, even though my brain was foggy with memory from our alone time upstairs.

Nora: *Hey, you. Maybe we could meet up today?*

I look at the text I sent to Asher over three hours ago, and flop back down onto my bed. After overcoming my anxiety and migraine episode, I was bored and on a Saturday, all I wanted to do was hang out with Asher. It was weird how much my life had changed in the span of six months; From spending no time with anyone to living in a palace and having a love interest.

But he hadn't answered. In fact, he hadn't reached out or responded in the two days since we'd been back from Vienna.

Had something else happened that I'd forgotten about? I

remember drinking too much and throwing myself at him, us going upstairs to be alone. Asher hadn't seemed like he'd been upset about anything, in fact I think he was uh ... pretty excited to be alone with a horny me.

Nora: *Hey, is everything okay?*

It's lame and makes me burn a little with desperation, but I've never had this sinking pit in my stomach. Before it was easy, having no one to answer to because I wouldn't allow anyone close enough to make me feel this way.

But I find that I hate it. Not knowing, wishing he would answer me. Running scenario after scenario in my head about what I could have done wrong and if he was ever going to want to talk to me again.

Jeez, I was pathetic.

Maybe ... I took my phone out again from where I'd hidden it between my pillows and brought up a new text message.

Nora: *Hey, would you want to do something today?*

I waited only moments before my phone buzzed with a response.

Eloise: *Sure, everyone else seems to be out of town for that horse race in Athens.*

I hadn't known about that event, nor had Asher told me he was going. Obviously, I couldn't ask Eloise about it without looking a certain way, and we weren't close enough yet for me to go to her for that kind of advice. But if he was there, and hadn't even asked if I was going, what could that mean?

Nora: *What should we do?*

    Eloise: *Well, I could really use a facial and a mimosa after how pissed I got in Vienna, let's go to my girl.*

I didn't know what she meant by her girl, but I wasn't about to suggest something like eat lunch in the park for fear of her telling me it was so beneath us. Even though I rather enjoy sitting by the pond in Hyde Park watching the ducks ...

Nora: *Sounds great, I'll meet you there in half an hour.*

After Eloise gave me the address and I freshened up a bit, the palace chauffeur took me over to the spa we'd agreed to meet at. And ten minutes after that, I was sitting in a chair next to Eloise in a white fluffy robe while tiny fish ate the dead skin off of my feet.

"This feels so ... weird. But oddly relaxing." I laughed as one of the fish nibbled my instep and tickled me.

"Stick with me, my little American, and you'll be a princess yet. I'll buff all of that chav out of you. After this we're getting facials, and then mud baths, and we'll finish off with a good blow out."

The lineup sounded a little more intimidating to me than relaxing, but I trusted Eloise as I watched her down her second mimosa. I had stuck with tea, not wanting anything clouding my judgment after the trip. Looking around at the gleaming white tile floors and white walls, trickling water pouring out of a large fountain covering one wall, I retracted my earlier statement about finally fitting in. Nothing about this spa day felt familiar or par for the course to me; in fact I felt like I was having an out of body experience. There was still some of that Pennsylvania girl left in me.

"So you stayed in Vienna a couple days after me?" I was

fishing but if I was nonchalant enough about it, maybe she wouldn't notice.

Eloise nodded, her blond hair wrapped high in a knot on her head. "I was a third bloody wheel to the Katherine and Drake drama. Whoever thought it would be a good idea for those two to shag should pour hot wax in their mouth."

I snorted. "That's a bit extreme."

"It's true though, they're both so unpredictable and insecure, it's like watching a wonky powder keg about to explode."

At first, I'm a little shocked she's talking about her friend that way, but then I remember that everyone in this world are just allies, not friends.

"What about you? Have you dated anyone at Winston?" Girl talk feels strange leaving my lips.

"Psh, absolutely not. High school boys are lame, and all of the ones at Winston are bloody spoiled. I like my men with a little street in them, don't forget where I came from now." She winks at me.

Sometimes I do forget we're cut from the same cloth. "So only bad boys then, huh?"

She smiles a devilish grin. "I suppose yes, but then we both know what that's like."

My stomach drops a little. "What do you mean?"

Eloise chuckles as the attendants move us to a different room and offer us more drinks. "Darling, Asher Frederick is just about the only boy I would date at Winston, if he wasn't such an arsehole. He's as bad boy as they come for the upper crust crowd, you must know that."

I suppose I did, but I didn't like where the conversation was going. "I guess so, but he's not that way with me."

"He's not that way with you, *now*."

Her words hit something inside of me, and of course she's

right. How easily I forget what he said and did before I'd softened up to him.

"Listen, I like Asher, he's the closest thing to a friend I have in this buggered world. But you need to be careful."

This seemed like more than an unneeded warning, and my skin began to prickle with awareness and dread. "Why is that?"

Eloise studied me before answering. "Listen, I don't know all of the details, but Asher's life has been pretty bloody awful. Sure, he's got money, but his family is ... harsh, to put it mildly. He's got some demons, and I've seen him be more calculating and cold than any other person I know. So just, be careful. I like you, new girl. I don't want to see you crash and burn."

As the facial person, or esthetician as Eloise corrected me, walked in, my phone buzzed.

Asher: *Hey, sorry my phone died. Want to go to the Alps next weekend?*

After Eloise's warnings, and two whole days of not hearing from him, I was weary.

But my first inclination was still to say yes.

*G*et your bloody head in the game, Asher.

That's what my father would say if he knew the kind of doubts and guilt I was having. In all honesty, I had no idea what was happening to me. I didn't second guess, I didn't feel bad. Those emotions and actions were for weak people, and the one thing I had been modeled not to do was be *that*.

Dreadfulness gnaws at my stomach as I watch Ed bully someone on the video game he's playing.

"You bloody wanker, I'll gut you!" He fires some kind of automatic weapon at his opponent's body.

"Do you have to yell?" I roll my eyes and go back to my phone, staring at the text messages Nora has sent over the past two days.

I haven't answered, and although I've been tempted, something changed for me that night in Vienna. Maybe it was because I'd taken care of her, instead of letting her embarrass herself. Or maybe it was because I was thinking about what might have happened if she hadn't gotten sick. The way her eyes had held so much heat and promise. Or maybe it was because of Evelyn and me pushing her away.

Probably a combination of the three, and other underlying feelings. I'd gone through my life an arrogant git, and now at the most critical time my conscience had raised its ugly head.

"Well mate, what do you want to do instead?" Ed throws down the controller, spreading himself over the big leather couch in the only room in my house with a TV.

"I don't know." I practically growl.

"What's got your knickers in a twist? You're as cuddly as a cactus today. Not that you're much better any other day of the week." He gives me a smarmy grin.

"If you're going to be a tosser, you can get out." I sulk on the big velvet glider next to the couch.

"Or I could just guess what's wrong. Hm, let's see ... it started about the time you took little miss princess upstairs at the opera, and came down looking like someone pissed on your toast." He taps his finger to his chin. "And now you are opting to hang out with me instead of being with her, which seems to be the only thing you do these days. Wait a minute! Did she break up with you? Did *Nora Randolph* break up with *you*?"

Ed is way too giddy in his supposed revelation, and it makes fury and bile crawl up my throat. "We're not even dating, you git. You know I'm not a big enough wanker to get feelings for some bird."

He laughs, his head tilting back like I've just told the world's funniest joke. "Come off it, mate. You like her, and you spend all of your time with only one girl. You're practically married."

I want to hurl that video game controller at his head. "Get out of my house."

"Nothing to be ashamed about, Asher. I actually rather like Nora, she's different."

And that word right there grates on my nerves even more. Because she is different, and I fancy her because of it.

"Listen, why don't you two kiss and make up, and then we can all go somewhere this weekend. How about Ibiza? The Canary Islands? Oh, we could go to Santorini ..."

I don't feel like listening to his little spoiled brat antics right now. Ed knew nothing about sacrifice or struggle, he'd grown up with not a care in the world and a silver spoon up his arse. Walking out, I took the stairs two at a time. He didn't bother to follow, for all I knew he was showing himself out or trying to nab some food from the kitchen staff.

There is a room at the end of the hall on the third floor of our brownstone that I never venture into. Sometimes locked, always with the door closed, it was my mother's room. The one that still houses her baby grand piano, dusted and maintained but never played. It hasn't played a note in ten years.

I'm not sure why, but today I keep going, I don't turn off into another room even when my stomach drops out, even when I feel like I might punch a hole through the door.

Slowly, I open it. I've only come in here twice since her death, but I strain to smell her scent. Lilies and vanilla, she was always so elegant and put together. But, just like her image, the scent has vanished from my mind. Nothing looks familiar, and I can't conjure up a memory of her sitting at the bench, practicing her playing in rhythm with the metronome.

As the years have progressed, I've been able to picture her face less and less. Sure, there are still the odd assortments of photographs I find myself mesmerized by, but if I sit in the dark and just think about my mother, it is exceedingly hard to recall her features. Her green eyes, the same as mine, her dark brown hair always perfectly done in one of those buns on the back of her neck. That tiny gold necklace she always used to wear, the one with the locket and her parent's pictures inside.

What I can remember, always toward the end of her life, was that deep, depressive sadness that sat in her eyes like a mourning veil.

The room is a light blue, with pictures of different blue flowers all over the wall. It's the only place in the house that still has some sort of feminine touch, and all of her keepsakes are still in here ... as if one day she'll be returning for them.

Sitting on the bench of the piano, I have to bite my fist to keep from screaming. I feel like someone coming unleashed, like the fabric of my soul is being torn apart and I can't decide which way to follow it.

Glancing up, my mother's picture stares back at me. She's young, probably caught in a moment in time before I was even born. In the photo, she's laughing on the beach, looking at something behind the camera.

I can't ever remember her that happy.

According to my father, shortly after I'd turned two she started her affair with Bennett McAlister. They'd been childhood sweethearts, and then she'd met my dad and fate had turned out differently. But once she'd seen Bennett again, it was all over.

I may not remember much about her life, but I was fully knowledgeable on her death. The way the papers reported her blood alcohol level, twice the legal limit to drive an automobile. They questioned why she'd been on the bridge that night, so late when no one even saw her make a splash into the frigid Thames. It wasn't until two hours later, when the men who cleaned up the streets of London, came out for their five a.m. route and saw the mangled metal where she'd driven over.

Resolve settles in my gut, and I know that I have to continue.

"Ed!" I yell, hoping he's still in the house.

"Yeah, mate?" he calls up the stairs.

"We're going skiing."

"Righto!"

Pulling out my phone, I finally open the messages I've been avoiding for two days.

Asher: *Hey, sorry my phone died. Want to go to the Alps next weekend?*

My travel education and passport have definitely gotten an upgrade over the last six months, but I had seen nothing in this world that compared to the Swiss Alps.

Rolling hills capped with snow, crystal valleys with lakes that held a mirror of the picture-perfect clouds. The freshest air I'd ever breathed, and gigantic pine trees that had probably graced the hills for far longer than anyone who was residing in them had been alive.

Even from the plane windows coming in, my breath had stood still in my lungs. It was as if God or the creator of this beautiful planet, depending on which theory you subscribed to, had put this monumental place here just for people to stop and awe at. And on the ground ... it was so much more.

The natural landscape was astonishing, and the upscale resort that Asher had booked only added to its charm. Dozens of log cabin buildings dotted the mountainside, the tall peaks rising up behind the beautiful little village. Korbier was apparently the most upscale, private ski resort in the Alps, and you could only make a reservation after a background and credit check, and three members vouching for your credentials. Naturally, the group of people I was with had no problem.

"We may need to start you out on the bunny hill, Nora." Ed winks at me as he passes through the sunporch with his plate of breakfast.

He, Asher, Eloise, Speri, and the twins, Lillian and Alexander, that I don't know as well are all staying in the villa. We got in late last night, my sense of direction and time kind of thrown off coming from rainy London to snowy Switzerland. I hadn't seen snow since last Christmas in Pennsylvania, and it brought the sense of homesickness rushing back.

The villa had eight bedrooms, all with private bathrooms that had sauna tubs and rainfall showers. It had six fireplaces, a game room, a hot tub, and a sun porch where I had spent almost every hour so far. The room was comprised solely of windows, and the natural light glistening off the snow made the mountain in full view look like some kind of gleaming Mount Olympus.

"You forget that I'm from one of the East Coast's prime skiing locations, and that I was on a snowboard before you were probably even sucking your thumb." I sip my coffee, not even turning to address him with my barb.

He snorts from the large arm chair by the fireplace in the corner. "Snowboard? How impoverished of you. And those are measly States mountains. You've never seen the Alps before."

I rolled my eyes, less than intimidated by him. "Just see if you can keep up."

While my time had mostly been spent in books and computers, I really did enjoy the winter season back home. I wasn't normally the athletic type of girl, but there was something holy about sliding down the side of a mountain, nothing but the wind in your hair and the cold biting at your face.

"Morning." Asher sits down across from me, his plate piled high with an English breakfast assortment.

He's been ... different, to say the least. I hadn't even hesitated to say yes to coming on this weekend trip, which could have not worked well in my favor. We haven't discussed those two days, or what happened at the opera. I didn't want to bring it up on the plane ride, where he was friendly but didn't sit in the seat next to me. And when we'd arrived, he claimed he was tired and took a room on the opposite side of the house from me.

I was trying to trap my questions and feelings inside as to not blurt them out, but I didn't know how long that would last.

"Good morning. Sleep well?" What I really want to ask is why he didn't at least try to come to my room.

Not that I'd ever done anything like that, let alone sleep with another person in a bed besides my mom, but we were teenagers on a trip alone. Since we'd started ... doing whatever it is that we're doing, we'd never once been on an overnight trip that gave us this opportunity. And now, when I thought he'd be jumping at the chance, he'd gone to bed like I was the least attractive girl on the face of the earth.

"I did, yeah. Can't wait to get on the slopes." He smiled, and I tried to search for some other meaning behind that.

"Nora, do you ski?" Alexander, who was actually quite nice and unassuming compared to this crew, looked to me.

"I snowboard actually, which I'm sure is a sin on these mountains, but I don't really change who I am."

That's a semi-lie, I've changed a lot since moving to Europe, and even more since beginning to hang out with Asher and his friends. Sometimes, I feel like I don't even recognize myself anymore. Accepting the invitation to come on this trip, and boarding the plane, that feeling only sank in further. But I made myself a promise as I laid awake last night, wondering about a stupid boy. I was too smart a woman to allow this world, the money and power and lust, change me. I promised myself that I would try to be my most authentic self from here on in.

Glancing across the table, I catch Asher's eye. There is something unreadable in those green pools, and I'm trying not to ask him what he thinks.

"All right, children … let's get a move on. I'm going to kick all of your arses out there on that snow." Ed runs upstairs to his room with all the grace of a toddler.

An hour later, after a stop in at the chalet for some pre-skiing hot apple cider and a tense lift ride, we all stand at the top of the mountain.

"I'm going to take the black diamond run, sissies. See you at the bottom!" Ed takes off, practically diving into the mountainside.

"We're going to stick to the green circle, thanks. Nora, you coming?" Speri and Eloise head for the easier run.

Lillian and Alexander are still on the lift, something about buying new boots. It's only us four, standing at the top with the question floating in the air.

"Actually, I'm going to board on the black diamond. But thanks!" I wave them off, and they shrug and start down the easier trail.

"So how about you, pretty boy?" I turn to him, finally alone for the first time in nearly a week.

He smiles, the first truly genuine one I've seen since Vienna. "This pretty boy is actually pretty good, if you didn't know. But then again, I'm doing the real winter sport. I'm not sure what that wonky board you're wearing is."

"Bet I can beat you to the bottom." I can't help but flirt, because the banter between us feels too good.

Asher moves closer. "I think that's a bet I just might need to take."

And without warning, he springs into action, sliding down the slope with the ease and grace of a skilled jungle cat. My muscles move, using their practiced pull and push to get my body into motion.

Once, I'm going, speeding down the mountain full force as I swing my hips and use my arms to balance. Snow flies up behind me, the cool unadulterated air filling my lungs.

At first, Asher is far away, using his skiing poles to propel him faster. But soon, I'm right on his tail, maneuvering around trees and snow drifts down the difficult course.

"Bloody hell!" Asher yells as I pass him, the gleeful smile painting my lips is one of pure happiness.

I'm in my natural element, and all of the worries and doubts about my life right now melt away. I don't think about the move or the wedding, the paparazzi or college or even Asher. I just let my feet glide along the white powder, the sun beating down upon my face.

As we near the bottom, he and I are neck and neck. I can practically taste the win, and even though I'm not usually a competitive person, I feel the burn of becoming a champion heat my blood.

Ed stands at the bottom, a couple of other resort-stayers watching as we speed down the slope.

But instead of Asher moving ahead of me, or me pulling out the last-minute win ... we crest to a stop at the exact same time.

"A tie ... so what happens now?" I wipe my brow, the adrenaline from the race coursing through me.

"I guess it means I buy you a drink." Asher shrugs, and I can't help but fall under his spell again.

"**I**t took a couple of hours, but I got you that drink."

Asher sets down the glass of wine in front of me, and I don't take my eyes from the large stone fireplace in the middle of the living room of the villa.

"You really didn't have to do that. I'm fine with my tea, kind of trying to lay off alcohol." I test the conversation between us, wanting to talk about the elephant in the room.

Dinner at the chalet was nice, the whole group got dressed up and had good conversation and even better food. Asher and I had made small talk, but it was still going on two days here and we hadn't addressed anything. And I felt it, the tension or whatever it was. Maybe I was building it up in my head, but I had always valued being up front and honest. I needed to get it all off of my chest.

He sits down on the couch with a foot of space between us. "I didn't think you drank that much anyway."

"Well, I made some mistakes in Vienna."

"I don't think you did." His tone of voice makes me think he's trying to avoid.

I needed to cut the bullshit. "Listen, Asher ... I'm still not super sure what happened in Vienna. I got drunk, I said some things, and I got sick. I'm not sure where in there we went wrong ... but I kind of thought we had something going. If not, you can correct me. And if you don't want to continue, then I'll accept that as well. But I don't want this awkwardness between us. You don't have to avoid me, and I apologize for whatever it is that I did. I just want to be an adult about it, because I do genuinely like you. Even if you were a huge arsehole when we met."

A smile spreads wide across his face. "Just when I think I've got you all figured out, you surprise me again, princess."

He hasn't called me that since Vienna, and it secretly makes bubbles of giddiness float up from my stomach.

"You didn't do anything wrong, by the way." Asher turns to me, his long, muscled arm on the back of the couch. I'm in a trance listening to his clipped British accent, the sound tickling my heart and between my thighs. "If anything, I'm wrong."

I try not to smile or feel any sense of hope, because maybe this conversation is only leading to the place where we don't continue what we are doing.

He looks at me in a deep sort of way, like he's trying to see my soul. "I wanted to be alone with you, you don't know how badly I wanted that. And when you got sick, I wanted to take care of you. That is what ... made me go a little bonkers to be honest. I'm not a one-girl kind of guy, Nora ... and I think you know that. I don't do caring or sensitive or nice. But with you, that's all I seem to want to do. It makes me a little wonky, makes that arsehole part of me want to rear its ugly head."

"I'm not asking for anything you don't want to give, I want to make that clear." I say it, but I want so badly for him to prove me wrong. To want to want the same things that I do.

"I know that, you never put any expectations on me. But you see, you make me want to be better, Nora. You make me want to have you put expectations on me. And that ... scares me. Jeez, I sound like a child."

"You kind of do." I promised I'd be authentic. "Asher, I like to be around you. I enjoy our banter and when we hang out. I even like when you kiss me." I blush, because I can't talk about being physical with him without getting embarrassed. "I'm new to all of this too, but I do know that I like you and only you. That I'm not afraid to say it or keep ... being together."

There, I'd been honest. My heart was pounding out of my chest as he sat on the other side of the couch, staring at me with those twinkling eyes.

"I want to be together with you too. Only you." Asher bridged the gap between us, his strong arms coming around me. "And I'll try not to be a bloody wanker."

I absolutely melt. "I guess that's all a girl could ask for."

His response is warm lips meeting mine, the fireplace crackling in the background as he stokes the embers inside of me. It's the first kiss we've shared in what feels like a lifetime, when in reality it was less than seven days.

Asher's mouth feels new, unexplored, and I am greedy as our tongues meet. He nips at my lip and I moan in surprise, the action catching me off guard but shooting straight to my core. Strong, callused hands wrap in my hair, pulling gently at the strands and moving to caress my neck. My skin is burning up, my fingers reaching to stroke his strong jaw and feel the muscles lurking beneath his black sweater.

"Come to my room. Please." Asher pulls away, leaving the invitation hanging between us.

The two sides of my brain wage war, debating whether it's smart to go or stay. But last night, this was all I had wanted ... and now it was staring me in the face. I felt it in my gut, this was it. All my life, I'd gotten feelings deep in my stomach about what was right to do and what was wrong.

And right now, going up to Asher's room with him was the right thing to do. "Okay."

Everyone was either out at the bar in the chalet, or in the hot tub outside. Quietly, Asher took my hand and led me up the stairs and down the hall to his room. We didn't talk or kiss on the way, but my skin prickled with anticipation. Where our fingers were locked, I could feel the underlying heat and need.

He pulled me gently inside and locked the door behind me. It was dark, but the white snow covering everything outside the window made everything glow with a light that only the moon could provide.

In that moment, I felt truly vulnerable for the first time in my life. "I'm not ... I've never ..."

Asher cuts me off, putting a finger to my lips. "We don't have to do anything you don't want to do."

I gulp, nodding against his hand. He leans in, kissing me again, and then we're moving. I grab hold of him, let him make the decisions because I'm not sure I can think with all of the arousal and anxiety buzzing around my head. The backs of my knees hit something solid, and I know that we're teetering at the edge of the bed.

Fingertips toy at the hem of my sweater, and I suck in a lungful of air.

"Relax. Is this okay?" His smooth accent purrs in my ear.

My nipples bud at his voice, and I nod into his shoulder. Slowly, so slowly that I have to hold my breath, Asher lifts my sweater up and away. The cool air of the room hits my bare skin, and I have an instinctual need to fold my arms across my chest.

"Let me see you." Asher's voice is husky as he prevents me from doing just that, reaching down and twining his fingers through both of my hands. Silently studying me, I feel his eyes trail over my simple navy bra and down toward the waistband of my jeans.

"I want to see you too." I don't realize I've spoken until his eyes shine bright with devious pleasure.

Asher's head tilts, those dark black locks shifting a bit, and then he pulls his sweater over his head with one hand gripping the fabric behind his neck. I'd seen him in his rowing uniform at the regatta, and then once after school when he'd been going to practice. But neither of those experiences had prepared me for this.

I'd also seen shirtless men before, even ones my own age. But those meant nothing compared to a real, live Asher in front of me ... the first boy who I'd really been attracted to naked just inches from my own shirtless body. His muscles looked as if they'd been carved into his flesh, his arms long and brawny from the hours spent in the boat. He had a little white scar running up his left shoulder, and his nipples were dark against his olive skin. Six perfectly sculpted ab muscles stuck out like bricks against his flat stomach, and I couldn't help but reach a finger out to touch them.

I'd never been alone, in a dark room, this close to a boy that made my heart beat out of my chest when he was around.

"You're beautiful." The simple words make my throat burn.

The need to clench my thighs together in my jeans is strong as Asher lifts me by the elbows to sit on the bed.

"Scoot back." He tells me as he starts moving onto his hands and knees, crawling up toward the pillows. With his dark hair and soundless movements, he's like a panther ready to strike on its naïve prey.

We both reach the top of the bed, and I rest my head on the fluff of pillows. Asher faces me, a streak of moonlight crossing his chest. I'm tingly and I feel like I can't take full breaths, my lungs won't hold the normal capacity.

His hand reaches for my cheek, and we meet in the middle, our kissing session from downstairs continuing on a deeper level. There is more speed involved, and when he moves his hands to my bare stomach, a single firework detonates in my stomach. It fizzes into every part of my body, and fills me with enough boldness to reach out both hands and palm the muscles on his stomach.

Asher hisses into my mouth, and I pull back, thinking I may have done something wrong.

"Keep them there." he growls, but his eyes are compassionate, and he dives back in for another kiss.

I put my hands back, exploring his warm flesh as our tongues dance and light the fire in between my legs. Before long, I'm squirming and I can't quite seem to stop. Asher's hands move up, sending goose bumps trickling across my skin. And soon, his fingertips play at the exposed skin of my breasts, wandering along the top of my bra cups in a teasing manner.

He pulls back, the question in his eyes. I nod, gulping because I know that I'm about to cross a line I've never ventured over before.

Painstakingly, Asher's fingers reach behind my back and undo my bra. I feel the straps loosen, the cups give. My nipples bud even tighter, and in a second they're exposed, seen by a man's eyes for the first time.

He palms them, rolling the buds in circular motions. The action makes me rub my thighs together and strain my neck, a moan involuntarily escaping my lips. I grab the skin in my hands tighter, and Asher moves his hips against mine. I can feel how aroused he is, the hard length of him pressing against the zipper of his jeans.

After a few minutes of kissing and fondling, it's not enough. I burn in a place I've never burned before, and I'm not even embarrassed by the noises I'm making. All air leaves the room when Asher reaches for the button of my jeans, but I don't stop him.

"I'm going to make it feel good, but it will hurt first." he whispers against my hair.

My body tenses, thinking I need to reciprocate the favor and not knowing how. I reach for his button, fumbling to undo it.

"No, let me do this first. I want to make you feel good, Nora." His voice is sincere, and makes me flush all over again.

I keep my hands on his stomach, and let him push my jeans over my hips and down. How he knows it will hurt, that I'm a virgin, I'm not sure. Maybe he guessed, or maybe it shows. The thought flits out of my head when his hand breaches my underwear.

Thick fingers feel around my core, pulling gently at the hair on my pelvis. I bury my head in his shoulder, suddenly self-conscious that I'm not bare like most of the girls my age. I just never thought to shave it, and now I don't know what he thinks.

"This is so sexy." Asher rasps into my ear, and a jolt of wetness burns through me.

His fingers travel south, stopping when he swirls the wetness at my core between them. Then he presses one long, dexterous finger against the swollen button, and I shudder with sweet relief. It feels incredible, out of this world, indescribable. His rhythm picks up, circling faster and with more pressure.

"Oh God ..." The words escape my lips.

"I'm not God, princess. But I can make you feel better than him."

A screech emanates from my throat when something invades me, pushes inside me. The burn mixes with pain, and pleasure circles around it. The two mix as Asher pushes his finger in deeper, a dam in me bursting. Slowly, the buzz of pain fades and a tidal wave of ecstasy follows it.

"Please ..." I don't know what I'm asking for, but Asher seems to know.

He slowly pulls the finger out, and then pushes it back in. I squirm, gripping his abs tighter. He continues the rhythm, slow and torturous, leaving me teetering on the edge of some kind of cliff.

I'm only half-conscious of Asher popping the button of his jeans open and pulling the zipper down, freeing himself. I watch in lustful awe as he tugs on himself, the thick erection in his hand turning my stomach inside out and making me burn even more as his finger plunges into me.

I want to make him feel the kind of pleasure he's making me feel. Tentatively, I reach down, covering his hand with my own. His eyes burn as my fingers touch his heated skin, the hardness not as solid as I thought it would be. It's more like velvet-wrapped steel, soft but rigid all at the same time. I circle my hand around his length, and stroke as I just watched him do.

"Bloody hell, Nora ..." His head drops into my hair as I do it again, and he adds a finger inside me.

I can't help but moan louder, which only makes him increase his rhythm. And that only makes me squeeze him harder, pull on him faster. It's like we're the fuel to each other's fire, and only our hands can light the matches.

Everything moves like a blur, fast but slow, sweet but sinful. I'm so close to something that I can taste it, and it feels like my skin starts to sing in a way. My toes curl, and everything inside of me - every nerve ending, hair, follicle - feels like it's going to combust.

A careening moan hits my ears, and I realize absently that it's from my own mouth. My whole body convulses with the orgasm that Asher takes from me, and I squeeze my eyes shut to focus on the intense pleasure coursing through my system.

"Christ!" Asher growls, and wetness coats my hand where I'm still stroking him. My lids fly open, and I watch his face as it contorts with relief and gratification.

As my ears stop buzzing from the pressure that my body lets

out, I realize that his fingers are still inside of me and my hand is coated in his pleasure.

"I didn't know." The thought must pop out of my mouth before I can stop it.

"Huh?" Asher sounds breathless.

I blush even though he's still touching the most intimate part of me. "I never understood what all of the hoopla was about ... until just now. That felt ..."

"I know." He smiles, kissing my cheek.

We clean up, with him handing me tissues and letting me use his bathroom. And when I go to leave, he pulls on my elbow and tells me to stay.

We don't talk about the fact that I'm a virgin, or that he's the first boy to ever touch me in that kind of way. He just gathers me in his arms under the covers and nods off.

I don't think I sleep more than an hour, my brain is so full of thoughts.

I key in the code to my locker, and let out a shriek when a balloon floats out and into my face. Something starts crowing, or singing ... I can't tell because I'm too flustered by the thing floating above my head.

"What the hell?"

"Happy Day of the Turkey!" Asher stands on the other side of my locker door, his arms spread wide and a genuine smile on his face.

Looking at the balloon floating on the ceiling, and finally being able to place the song, Arlo Guthrie's "Alice's Restaurant." Laughter bubbles up from my throat until I'm hunched over in amusement.

"Do you mean Happy Thanksgiving?" I say between breaths.

His green eyes falter, but the spark is there. "Well, whatever ... you knew what I meant. But yes, we don't celebrate here, and I know how much you like your locker decorated."

Suspicion pulls at my insides, back to the first day when Miley Cyrus had sang from my American-flag decorated locker.

"Was it you who put that stuff in my locker on the first day of school?" I eye him cautiously.

He laughs. "I may have charmed the ladies in the front office to give me your combination. Although being me, it's never hard to get what I want."

"Yeah, we'll see about that." I rolled my eyes, and he tickled my ribs. "You know, that really humiliated me."

Asher looks repentant. "And I've been trying to make up for how big of an arse I was." Bending down, he wraps his hands around my waist and whispers in my ear. "I hope I've been doing a good job."

My body flushes, because I know he has been working diligently, with his hands and mouth, to make it up to me. My mind flashes to the other night in the recreation room of his house, where he'd undressed me on the couch and made those noises come out of my mouth again.

"You have. But I'm not letting you off the hook just yet." We may have gained a lot of ground back in Switzerland, but my self-preserving nature still sat firmly locked in place.

One of the girls who had approached me in the hallway when Asher and I had first started seeing each other stares at us, jealousy burning her through her eyes. I wasn't usually the kind to search for attention or gratification, but her comments had pissed me off. The way she felt she should know my personal business, as if I was open fully for all of Winston to gossip about.

And Jesus Christ, I'd just realized it. For months it hadn't sunk in, because being attached to Bennett was one thing. But back home, in school, I could have been invisible for how much the other students noticed or talked about me.

And I realized ... I was popular.

It was such a trivial, narcissistic thing to be proud of, but when you've never had it before, the adrenaline it shot your blood up with was addicting. I'd loathed the popular crowd, especially those here at Winston because money was everything and technically none of the money I had now was mine. But when you were actually on the inside ... the view from the top was heady.

I leaned into Asher and kissed him gently, the song still playing behind us. I heard the girl's quick footsteps away from us as she caught up with a friend down the hall, their side eyes directed right at me.

"You know, we Brits aren't huge into PDA." He doesn't let me go.

"Well, too bad you're dating an American then. So, did you get me some cranberry sauce?" We start to walk down the hall, the day over.

"I'm going to be honest, I have no idea what that is."

The winter air is chilly, but not terrible as we push open the front doors. I wrap my fleece cape, a gift from Bennett, around my shoulders, and Asher just buttons his blazer. He told me once that from being on the frigid water so much for rowing, he is never truly cold.

"It's this kind of jelly that comes in a can, and you slice it up."

"Yuck." He makes a face as he latches his fingers in mine.

My heart speeds up, the gesture so touching and intimate. I never thought I'd be one of those girls, the ones who turned to mush when a boy talked or looked at them. But Asher is apparently my kryptonite.

"Says the guy who eats Yorkshire pudding and mince pie." I shudder at the thought of eating either.

He rubs his stomach as he hails a taxi. "God, I can't wait for Christmas feast. Or Boxing Day for that matter."

Opening the door, he ushers me in. "Where are we going?"

"You'll see. I may be able to find you some cranberry sauce after all."

His spontaneous nature is one of the things I admire most about Asher. One would think that someone with as rigid an upbringing as he had would tend to follow rules and act in accordance. But I've found, in the time we've spent together, that he is actually very go-with-the-flow. An adventurer with a calm nature about him, Asher is the perfect balance against my anxious personality. I never worry when I'm going anywhere with him, because I know that if things don't go as planned, he'll still make it fun for the both of us.

"I didn't even realize it was Thanksgiving." Strange, since it was one of my favorite holidays back home.

"It's because no one was talking about it." His profile is like a historic statue.

"Back home, Mom and I would bake all kinds of pies for just the two of us. We'd buy deli slices of turkey and make sandwiches, and leave all the room in our stomachs for pie. Apple, pumpkin, chocolate, pecan ... any kind we could fit in the oven."

Thinking about those memories makes me sad. This year, we'd be in a new place for the holidays. Already we'd forgot one, and we'd also have Bennett. We'd have to make new memories.

"That sounds nice." Asher squeezes my hand, and I know he's trying to lift me out of my funk.

The car comes to a stop and a mischievous glint comes into his eye.

"Who even said I had time to go gallivanting with you today?"

"I love it when you use big words. Come on, princess." He takes my hand and leads me up to an official looking building.

It's the same make and model as almost every building here; imposing and beautiful in its craftsmanship. The columns of white stone reach high up into the sky, and ornate windows and gargoyle statues are carved into the sides. Asher ducks us into what I think is a doorway, but on second glance, is actually an archway.

I can't help but gasp.

"What is this place?"

Staring up, I take in the high ceiling made of glass, the arches formed by columns at every store front. The alley that looks like something out of a Harry Potter novel, with its Victorian architecture so beautiful and prominent.

"Welcome to Leadenhall Market, one of my favorite places to come and hide out for an afternoon." Asher takes my hand and leads me under the giant archway and into a maze of shops, outdoor seating, and people milling about.

"This place is amazing. See, I thought we had big flea markets back home, but nothing near as gorgeous as this."

"A 'flea' market?" Asher swishes the words around in his mouth, not sure if they're good or bad.

I laugh at his sour expression. "Pretty much the same as this ... lots of vendors selling their own foods or goods. But nowhere near as upscale. Typically, it's held in a big field, with stalls separating the sellers."

Asher still looks confused, so I pat him on the back. "You know what, never mind. So, where do we go first?"

He smiles, a little mischievously, and pulls me toward a door. "I love this place, come on."

It's not turkey and mashed potatoes, but we start off with a cheese tasting that makes me want to groan. I've never had cheeses so creamy or delicious. Brie and cheddar with relish jelly and things I can't even pronounce, but they're so good that I never want to leave.

Eventually we do, venturing into a store kitty-corner from the cheese shop.

"They have some of the most amazing Korean pork you'll ever eat in your life."

I cock my head to the side. "I didn't realize your food tastes ranged so far outside the box."

"What, you think just because I attend all those stuffy steak dinners that I don't have a palate?" He fakes looking wounded.

"Well ... yeah." I can't help but chuckle. "It's nice to know you have some street sense in you. I love any kind of Asian food, but haven't been able to venture out much for it while I've been here."

"Then allow me, princess."

The store clerk prepares us a mini-sandwich each, loaded with Korean pork and red onion and purple cabbage. He squirts on a dash of spicy looking sauce and my mouth starts to water. We take our sandwiches outside, sitting at the tables under the glass dome and people watching.

"Oh my God." I can't help but exclaim.

"Good, right?" Asher says with a mouthful.

I nod, and a piece of the sandwich falls right out of my mouth and onto my chin. I blush horribly, embarrassed that I look like an animal devouring the fantastic creation in my hand. Asher just chuckles, leaning over and licking the bite off my chin. Then his lips travel higher, until they land on my mouth, giving me a spicy kiss.

"That's even better than my sandwich. Here, give me yours." He smiles with his eyes closed as he pulls away.

My heart dips and flops over, defeated from his charm and mouth.

After our sandwiches are finished, we hit a couple more stores, looking at vintage T-shirts with old band logos on them, and others with things like artisanal soaps and wines from all over Europe. Hand in hand, we walk the entire market, not bustling about or in a hurry to get anywhere. It's one of the best days I've had since we moved to London, and it's spent doing virtually nothing but eating and chatting with Asher.

By the end of the afternoon, and a cranberry pudding later, I'm leaning my head against Asher's shoulder in a taxi back to the palace. Neither of us talks, because the silence is companionable and there are no words necessary in this moment. I'm more comfortable here, with his arm around my shoulder, protecting me as the car weaves through end of day London traffic, than I have been almost anywhere in my life.

I've said it before, but I never knew much about what I wanted. Sure, I've always been smart, but I've never had a clear path of where I've wanted that to take me. I've never had a close group of friends, more have I really sought one out. There's never been a real need for me to be a fighter or a peacemaker, or make much of a decision about anything.

But being with Asher, it's the first thing that I've actively wanted. The thing I've felt a need for, yearned for, craved. And while it scared me immensely, it also emboldened me. Lit a fire in my belly and made me want to try my hardest at this ... harder than I'd ever tried at anything before.

There was also a calming sense that came over my body, in times of peace like right now. Everything at this moment was right in the universe, and I wasn't going to fight it one bit.

The holiday season in London has always been a time for great jubilee. Parties and seasonal cheer and everyone singing carols.

Bloody shit, I hated it. In our house, it was always a gloomy couple of months, overshadowed by my mother's death and my father hitting the liquor cabinet extra hard.

But this year, I had to pretend. Put on my knit green and red sweater and fake my love for Christmas movies and hot cocoa with marshmallows. All because Nora and I were together, really together, and I was homing in on my final step.

"You know I've never attended this stupid thing, and I'm only doing it for you." I pull on the bowtie at my neck, annoyed that I have to yet again squeeze into a tuxedo.

It was true, I'd never gone to the Winter Ball at Winston, but I was going this year simply because Nora had never been asked to a dance.

"Thank you for asking me. And for putting up with festivities, I know how much of a Grinch you are."

"I'll be even grinchier if you make me watch that incessant Jim Carrey in a fat green suit one more time."

"I used to wish I could live in Whoville when I was younger." She fastens an earring in and spritzes some bottle from her dresser on her neck.

I'm now a regular visitor at Kensington Palace, after our successful trip to Switzerland over a month ago. That night in my bedroom not only secured her and put her faith in me back on solid ground, but it had also been one of the hottest nights of my life. There was something sexier than shagging a woman when it came to Nora. Her innocence, her tentativeness when I undressed her, the way she'd unraveled as she orgasmed into my hands. God, I was hard as a fully-cocked shotgun each time I thought about it.

And the first time she'd gone down on me, just a week ago, keeping her eyes locked on mine for directions ... well I about lost it a second into her wrapping her lips around my shaft.

"Does this look all right?"

Nora shifts her feet in front of me, looking to see if I deem her worthy of going to the dance with me. Even though she had more brains than our entire school put together, and could be the sassiest mouth I'd ever engaged with ... there was still this schoolgirl insecurity that made her so appealing.

She shimmered like a real live snowflake, the long silvery column dress hugging her slim figure. Her red hair curled up on top of her head, looking like ringlets of fire falling down onto her cheeks.

"You look ... edible." I rise from her desk chair and walk across her room, bending down to bite the tip of her nose.

"Sweet." She rolls her eyes, and I wish we could stay here and I could show her just how edible she really is.

We walk down the stairs of the palace apartment together, my arm a balance for her in her high heels. My head is on a swivel, as it always is when I'm here, tracking Bennett. Tonight though, he and Rachel are in Canada on official business, something Nora told me when she was upset that her mom couldn't be there to see her off for her first school dance.

I've only seen Bennett once in my visits to hang out with Nora, and that time, just like at the regatta, he didn't recognize who I was. He still didn't realize that the son of his mistress was the one with his hands and lips all over his stepdaughter. And each time I entered the space he called home, I burned with the fury of knowing that he lived the life of a prince while my mother was cold in her grave.

Nora's chauffeur took us over to Winston, which was decorated with its traditional Christmas trimmings. The school spared no expense in its decor or Winter Ball budget, and when we walked into the auditorium, it looked like one of the grandest halls in London itself. White and silver fake snow, green and red curtains hung like a canopy from the ceiling, chiavari chairs and a full on buffet with food choices from all over Europe.

"I spiked the punch." Drake walked up to us, his eyes already drowsy with drink.

Nora hit his shoulder. "Why did you have to do that? You're incorrigible."

She and Drake had a banter between them that I didn't understand, but they had a riot keeping it up.

I squeeze Nora's hand where it's threaded in mine, and Speri walks up and glances at the gesture between us. My group of friends has been weirdly supportive of our relationship, not that we talk about it all that much. They know we are together, and they give us our space. I thought they would have been teasing or suspicious, but that's just my paranoia. No one, not even Ed, knows the real reason that I'm with her.

But I guess they'll find out soon enough.

"Could this band be any more boring?" Speri huffs, and we all look at the twelve-piece band playing some classical song.

"Ed, go flirt with the violinist and ask her to play some Rihanna, or at least Katy Perry," Katherine jokes.

The place is packed with Winston students of all ages, and I can't help but wonder how my life would have been different if I'd grown up with two happy parents like most of my classmates. Would I have come to this formal every year? Would I have had a steady, healthy relationship? Would I be blissfully ignorant like all of these bloody people?

"Ouch." Nora lets go of my hand, I realize I was squeezing the circulation out of her fingers.

"Sorry, love. Want to get something to drink?" I want to get her away from my group of friends.

As what I knew would be the end of our relationship loomed nearer, I wanted to cut off her contact from the group as much as possible. I wanted her left with no lifelines, no one to turn to. By hurting her as much as humanly possible, I would hurt *him*. The acid in my stomach churned ever more rapidly.

"So, what is the most favorite Christmas present you ever received?" Nora put her hands on my hips as I sipped the water bottle I'd picked up out of the bucket.

"I don't know." I shrug and look around the dance floor, avoiding her question.

"Oh, come on … you have to have a favorite. An electronic dog? No, you grew up rich. What, the Maserati you got when you were twelve?" She chuckles.

Nora is completely comfortable with me now, caught exactly where I want her in my crosshairs. Which makes it ever more difficult for more. On one hand, I've accomplished what I wanted to. But on the other, it came with something I wasn't expecting at all. I actually have real feelings for this girl. I thought I would be able to deflect them, to guard myself from the emotions that would come along with spending so much time with someone. But I'm not immune … and now I care about her. I find myself trying to make her laugh, or craving her touch when we're in a room full of people.

I think hard, tapping my finger to my chin. "Fine ... when I was eight I got a guitar. A Martin Vintage, made in nineteen twenty-six. It was beautiful, all polished wood and perfectly tuned acoustic strings. I spent hours trying to play that thing, perfecting songs on it."

"I didn't know you played an instrument." Her smile is smitten with my revelation.

"Yeah, my mum tried to teach me, she was the one with the musical gene." My hands froze where they'd been rubbing her back.

"Does she still play?" Nora's voice is small, and she knows that I haven't mentioned my mother before.

Someone laughs in the background as the band switches songs. The different noises of the ball filter in and out of my ears, and rage simmers in my veins thinking about the role her new family played in my mother's death.

"No, she doesn't." I don't elaborate.

We're interrupted by someone coming over the loud speaker. "And now, it's time to crown the annual King and Queen of the Winter Ball! You voted all week for your favorite classmates, and now it's time to see who you all think is the most beloved couple here at Winston!"

Everyone in the room turns toward the stage, and I can't help but grumble my annoyance. While I may be one of the "popular" kids here, I could not be more removed from the politics and gossip of the school. I'm so aloof that for some wonky reason, it makes people want to know more about me than if I were involved.

"And your King and Queen of this year's Winter Ball are ... Asher Frederick and Nora Randolph!"

The room erupts into applause, and my stomach turns to

bile. I hadn't even realized that so many people in this spoiled playground knew we were together, but apparently I didn't fly as under the radar as I had hoped.

"What?!" Nora's face was pure glee, while inside I was panicking.

She grabbed my hand and started walking to the stage, and I followed with numb limbs. I walked up the stairs, waited while they put the crown on her head and then put one on mine.

Looking at her, standing next to me in her queen's fashion, I could just imagine the gaudy thing cracking and falling to the ground. Just like I was hoping her life would do when I finally exposed the McAlister name and all of the atrocities he'd committed.

24

The definition of genius is one who has exceptional intellectual or creative power or other natural ability. And where do they collect geniuses?

Mensa.

I tested into the high IQ society when I was only eight, scoring in the whopping hundredth percentile on a standard IQ test. I was written about in textbooks, secured a corner of the local paper, and was called upon by university heads and scholars to visit their facilities. Once there, I was given math problems, science theories, legal hypotheticals and other categories in which they quizzed my knowledge. My brain was studied through MRI machines and CAT scans; medical professionals wanted to try to pinpoint the source of my intelligence. Said they'd never seen anything like me.

For all of the travel and voluntary testing I went through, we were compensated. Very well, actually. One university had given me a grant that would fully fund my college studies when it came time. Another paid my mother a lump sum just to have me sit in on lectures for a week and give my theories, of which fascinated the professors who attended.

It wasn't until about puberty that the headaches and anxiety came on. Doctors could never find the answer, or the cure, to why my brain seemed to overload itself. One second I would be fine, doing my homework at the kitchen table, and another I'd be doubled over in pain. Cluster migraines, they'd diagnosed, that seized my cranium, temporarily took my vision, and left me down and out for a week.

They always came on around times of testing, and I started to notice a pattern.

So today, as I'm studying for midterms at Asher's house, and my hand begins to shake, I can't help it that I drop the water glass I'd been about to drink from.

The glass shatters on the hardwood of his living room floor, and he jumps. "Are you okay?!"

He looks surprised, worry creasing his handsome face, but I can't move. My heart rate shoots up like a nonstop elevator to the top floor. I can feel the familiar pressure crawl up and over my chest like a lion ready to pounce, and the breath wheezing in and out of my lungs. My hands shake, the back of my neck becoming cold and clammy. The only word that I repeat over and over in my head is *no*.

"No, what? Nora?" Asher practically leaps off of the couch where he was lying down reading, and crouches next to me on the floor.

I must be saying it out loud, but I can't stop. I rock, willing the beast of anxiety to get off of my chest, to let me go.

"Love, what's wrong? Do you need ... should I call your mom? An ambulance?"

His hands come up to frame my face, and his warm touch helps to ease a bit of the pressure from my lungs.

"Anxiety ... attack. I ... I get them." I concentrate on breathing through the words, still rocking as he positions his body protectively around mine.

"What can I do? How do I—"

Asher sounds helpless, and his fear only makes the attack ripping through me get worse. My vision starts to spark and dim at the corners, so I grab his arms, throwing myself against his body. I've never tried the weight technique, would never let Mom spend the ridiculous amount of money it costs to buy one of those special blankets.

But I don't have my mom here, or my normal medicines. And if I get up and walk out on unsteady legs, he'll only follow me.

So I do the one thing I have at my disposal. I use *him*. "Hold ... me."

As if he's a surgeon jumping to work, Asher's arms lock around me. His legs lock around mine, putting us in a pretzel twist as I sit shaking in his lap. Squeezing as hard as he can, his lips comes to my ear.

"I've got you. I'm right here, Nora."

He's anchoring me to the ground, keeping me from trying to rip out of my own skin as the anxiety ripples from my brain to my toes. The weight of his body around me as my nervous system goes haywire actually feels ... calming.

Slowly, I can feel the air begin to fully fill my lungs, the feeling in my fingers where they clutch Asher's shoulders tingles back to life. I exhale, laying my head in the crook of his neck, my brain settling down and all of the thoughts that left me stranded in the dark go back into their black box of doom.

He loosens his grip, gently rubbing circles onto my back as I wipe away the tears I didn't realize were falling.

"If you wanted to get in my lap, you didn't have to fake an anxiety attack to do it." His voice is a whispered smile as he continues to hold me.

I can't do much but smile back into his shoulder. That was possibly the most embarrassing thing that has happened between us thus far, and he's joking about it while comforting me. Rather than running in the opposite direction as I melted down before his eyes, Asher stayed.

"Do you need anything? Need me to call anyone?" He had yet to move from the position we were in.

I cleared my throat, finally feeling confident enough to speak. "Some water, maybe. But ... just another minute."

I didn't want him to let go.

"What ... how do they happen? If you want to tell me." His lips pressed to my forehead.

I kept my head in his neck, smelling his unique, sophisticated scent. "My brain ... well, I think you know that it's ... different. The only explanation that doctors could ever come up with is that because I can digest so much information, my system, it kind of overloads. All of the information, all of the knowledge, just kind of gets me so worked up that I can't control it and the anxiety hits me like a full on tidal wave."

Asher holds my neck but slowly eases me out of his chest so that those jewel-like green eyes are staring straight into mine. "Well, I'll keep you anchored. I'm good with boats, if you didn't know."

Internally, my nerves are shot. I can't believe that actually just happened in front of him. It begins to sink in just how bad that attack could have gotten, and all of my past insecurities come to the forefront.

"You're not ... freaked out?" My voice is small and embarrassed.

This is really the reason I never let anyone get too close. It was bad enough that the kids back home, from the time I was accepted into Mensa until I left for London, thought I was a freak. I hadn't been good at masking my intelligence at first, and through elementary and middle school was a bit of a know it all. It wasn't until high school that I realized I was utterly alone because my peers were suspicious and paranoid of me. I was too this or too that for my own good, and they wanted nothing to do with me.

If they had known about the breakdowns too? I would have been a bigger pariah than the mayor who had been caught embezzling from the food bank.

Someone finding out about my attacks and migraines was my biggest fear. They left me so exposed and raw, I never thought that anyone besides my mom would accept me after watching the way my body broke down.

Yet here was Asher, being the exact opposite of the person I assumed him to be. He'd slashed all of my opinions about the kind of man he was. My heart spun with the realization, and for the first time in a long time, I felt the hard concrete around my heart fall away.

"Why should I be? It's not like it's something you can help, love." He pushes a lock of hair away from my face, and kisses my damp brow.

He was right of course, but my condition had always made me feel defective in a way. "Thank you for just ... helping me through it."

"This is why you freaked out on me that day in class when I told everyone how many answers you'd gotten correct, isn't it?"

"Yes." I'd forgotten my blow up at him.

"I never did apologize for that. I'm sorry for being a wanker, it was an arse move. If I had known what came along with being able to just click that well with academics, I never would have done it."

Reaching up, I placed my hand on his strong jaw, feeling the rougher skin there from where he'd shaved. My lips found his, plying at them and nibbling like he'd taught me to. My stomach dropped into my feet as I felt him start to swell where I still sat in his lap.

My brain knows that the weight of his body pushing against my skin was the healing technique that helped me come down from the attack. But my heart, the organ that seemed to turn to mush anytime it was around this boy nowadays, never wanted to survive another episode without him.

I was beginning to rely on Asher far too much. And though I was smart enough to know I shouldn't, I couldn't help the skyscraper fall I was taking for him.

The comfort of his arms made me sure of the path we were going down, and I was afraid that if either of us asked for more, I wouldn't be able to say no.

S ludge coats my stomach and the poison that is my blood at this point seems to be sickening me from the inside out.

My actions are finally catching up to me. Because as resigned as I am to destroying her stepfather, it makes me nauseous to think about what this will do to Nora. It was the New Year, and that was supposed to bring about change and resolution.

After what I'd seen the anxiety do to her, the way it ripped through her and bulldozed her faculties, I thought that maybe, just maybe, I didn't have to go through with it. Maybe I could stop it all, just keep being with her and try to live my life normally.

"That's it, just like that." My arms moved in tandem with hers, and her small hands were dwarfed by my own.

We moved together, the water lapping around us. The vibrations of our movement sound off of the aqua tiled walls, the stained glass sparkling with the ripples of the pool.

My father had this indoor training center built in the basement of our townhouse when I'd first shown real promise in rowing at the age of ten. The pool was half of an Olympic regulation size, and had a stationary rowing boat that could be harnessed in the middle of the water to practice oar skills and build leg strength.

That's where Nora and I sat, in our bathing suits, her nestled between my legs as I taught her how to properly steer a boat.

"You don't want to row too hard or too soft, once you get in the rhythm, you'll feel it."

She nods, intent on getting this right. "And once I get it, I'll steal your position as Stroke."

Loving her cheekiness, I press my lips to her neck to distract her. "You're not the one who will be stroking."

Having her this close to me in a wet bathing suit doesn't do much for my hardening knob.

"Is it ..." Her voice trails off.

"What?" I continue to kiss her neck, and feel her skin heat under my palms.

"I know that you know ... that I haven't ..." She stops rowing and the oars float aimlessly in the water.

I feel her hesitation. "Shagged someone? It isn't a sin to say the word sex, princess."

"Don't mock me, I'm already embarrassed as it is. Well, yes, I haven't. But I just ... is it better than what we already do?"

I nearly swallow my tongue, because talking about sex with her without actually doing the deed will be exceedingly hard.

"I'm sorry, love ... it's just not as taboo as you think. It's not better I'd say, just different."

Nora turns, her hazel eyes seeking mine. "How many people have you slept with?"

I try not to choke on the awkward cough that reaches my throat. "I don't want to talk about things or people that no longer matter."

And I didn't need to divulge the large number of women I'd bedded, it would only serve to make her dwell on the scoundrel I'd been ... and still was.

"I think ... no, I know that I'm ready." Her voice is confident as she turns around in the boat, kneeling to face me.

I haven't brought up sex to her at all, feeling guilty enough for a month that I'd eventually have to ruin her innocent delusions that I was a good boyfriend. But it didn't mean I didn't think about ... didn't want it when my mouth was between her legs and she was thrusting her fingers into my hair. She always looked so beautiful and pure, like a white flower that I was soiling with my dirty soul.

"We don't have to do this." I try to protest as she sets her small hands on my thighs, her touch shooting straight to my balls.

"I want to. I'm ready. I trust you."

You shouldn't. I think it, but don't say it as she covers my mouth with hers. As the months have gone by, she's become more confident in taking control of the physical side of our relationship, of initiating. She knows it drives me especially bonkers when she straddles me, controlling the kiss and the pace.

And that's what she does now, in the boat in the middle of my indoor pool. I can't help but lean back, cradling her against me as the water rocks all around us. Nora's hips grind against me, her core lined up right against my cock. I grind my hands into her bum, gripping the firm skin and pushing it hard down onto me.

The boat begins to tip as our snogging intensifies, and Nora breaks it off with a laugh. "I'm not sure we can do this here."

I push back a wet strand of her scarlet hair, and sign my death certificate. I'm too randy and ready to go to say no, and she wants me to be the man who takes her virginity. If I say no, she'll leave now and my plan will be ruined. But if I say yes, it will be the ultimate mark of shame on my soul when she finally finds out what I was doing all this time. If I do this, she'll never speak to me again after it all falls down.

"We should do this properly, in a real bed where I can look at you."

She sucks in a breath and her eyes swim with something that looks very close to a word I shouldn't even be thinking.

We swam to the stairs, me hot on her tail as she walked out, water sluicing off of her body. I'm so torn, guilt roiling in my gut, but I won't stop. Can't. She's too pure and radiant, and I'm too big of a prick.

All alone in my house, we wind the steps up to my bedroom together, my hands on her hips as she walks in front of me. She's confident, nothing shaky about her resolve to give me one of the greatest gifts she'd ever give anyone. Something in me wants to be better, try harder for her. I want to make this memorable for her, not to tarnish anything just yet.

Soon enough, she would hate me. But for now, I could do this. I could be the man she thought I was.

"You're sure, Nora?" My voice shakes as we enter my bedroom, because I'm not bloody sure at all.

"I trust you. I want this to be with you. Only with you." She moves toward me, her wet suit hitting my naked chest as she presses up on her toes and lays a gentle kiss on my lips.

In the back of my mind, I wish that I was only hers too.

Her skin is hot and flushed against the coolness of her wet bathing suit, and I peel it down, removing it like a second skin from her body. She's all small curves and long lines ... her tits just a handful each, my thumbs pressing against those nipples that always seem to be ready just for me. Nora lets out a sigh and I wish that I could record that sound, play it on a loop in my head for hours. My mouth is hot and greedy on her cool skin, and I trail kisses from her neck down over her collar-bone, over one breast and then the other. The action works me up, my cock hardening painfully in my still wet swim trunks.

"Mmm, yes ..." Nora's whisper hits my ears as my lips cross the invisible line at her hips.

Her body vibrates with arousal, and I fear that if I do what I want to in this moment, she won't be able to stand. Gently, I push her back toward my big king bed, and lift her up and onto it so that she's sitting with her feet dangling over.

And then I travel down, planting an open mouth kiss on her wetness.

Nora lets out a sharp wail, and I wish I could watch her face the whole time I feast on her because just the sounds are driving me out of my mind. She's sweet and pure, like unfiltered honey. I lap at her, my blood boiling to the point of explosion, my cock thick and painfully throbbing in my shorts. I release myself, my thumb sweeping over the wetness already collected at the head.

"I ... want ..." She starts to reach down, taking her juicy core away from me.

Her small hands grip down my body, as if she is going to return the favor. I lift her back up, planting her securely on the bed.

"No, this is about you."

It has to be about her. If I let her do anything for me right now, pleasure me or make any second of right now directed toward me ... I don't know if I could keep from breaking down. I have to give her this, sacrifice before I break her world in two.

"Then I want you, all of you." Her face is earnest, not a shred of doubt or fear crossing in her eyes.

My soul twinges, knowing that evil lurks just around the corner and that I'm going to bring the sky falling down on her head. But I push the thought out, also knowing that I can't stop now even if I tried. She's perfect, lying there beneath me as I crawl over her body, reaching to my drawer for a condom.

My wet bathing suit hits the ground with a thud, and Nora arches her back, her tits pushing into my chest as I pinch the head of my cock.

"You tell me if I hurt you. Tell me to stop." I wish she would, right now. I wish she knew it all, and that she'd slap me across the face right now and leave.

"I trust you." The way she says it, she might as well have said those four little letters that can bring a man to his knees.

The twinkling rays of midday sun beat through the room, her hazel eyes shining up at me so clearly. She doesn't cover herself, doesn't shy away. Nora is a completely different being than I ever assumed, and in the back of my mind, I repeat those four little letters.

I don't dare say them.

I fist myself, positioning at her entrance. Sweet, fiery burn runs through my veins, making me high on Nora. That first push, the first suction of her on me ... it chokes me. Grabs me by the throat and won't let me breathe properly.

I've been with other girls, slept with models and princesses and girls who would blow any man's bloody mind. But I never realized how empty those nights all were. How lazy I'd been, how much I was letting those girls and those moments pass me by. And it hits me ... I've never felt this way about any girl. About anyone. She could destroy me, already has, and doesn't even know it.

Nora is so tight that I have to clench my teeth, use every ounce of strength in my body to keep from coming. Inch by inch, I cant my hips, thrusting so slowly inside of her.

"Ah!" Nora cries out when I'm about halfway in, twinges of pain crossing her face.

"I'm going to push all the way in." I hold her face in my hands. "It will only hurt for a minute."

I don't give her time to digest this information, I just push, fully sheathing myself in her. A pained scream tears from her lips, and I swallow it, covering her mouth with mine.

I suck and nibble at her lips, coaxing and heating them ... my heart rate notching even higher as she starts to respond. Nora breaks our kiss, breathing into my mouth as she wiggles her hips, testing out how we felt connected.

My cock twitched inside of her, making me clench my arse to keep it together. "You can't move like that or this will be over way too soon."

"It feels so ... good." Her whisper tickles my ear.

That sets me off, a jolt of electricity racing down my spine. I move, dragging out and thrusting back in slowly. Nora moans, her eyes rolling back as I bottom out inside of her. My hips move of their own accord, repeating the motion, building us both up to the inevitable cliff we would fall back down.

"*Asher ... Asher ... Asher.*" Nora chants my name over and over, the word dropping like fuel to my rhythm with each syllable.

I've never worried about the pleasure of my partner, about whether or not she came at all. But I told Nora this was about her, and I wasn't lying. For once in my life, I hadn't lied.

"Get there, Nora ... I want to feel you." I suck on her neck, earlobe, jaw.

Her moans come closer together, everything in her beginning to tighten.

I feel it, when she unravels, when her body spasms and clutches at mine. When she talks in half-sentences, the walls of her core gripping me. And I can't hold back any longer, my cock pummeling into her as her eyes latch onto mine. Staring at me, like she's seen another universe that only she and I exist in.

I combust, blasting apart with such force that I can't catch my breath, can't figure out which way is up. My world spirals, ecstasy coursing through my flesh with Nora's eyes the only thing grounding me.

She's going to hate me.

It's the last thought I have before I collapse into her shoulder, smelling her hair and wondering what the hell I'd done.

As I'd sat down at the grand dining table in their apartment at Kensington Palace, Bennett still didn't recognize me.

It was the first time I'd been invited over for dinner with the whole family, and it was surreal finally sitting across from the man who had ruined my father's life. His soon-to-be wife sat next to him, looking adoringly into his eyes as he told some bloody story.

Nora listens on with interest, and they both laugh when he gets to the punchline. I follow suit, not having heard a word over the blood whooshing in my ears. I'd spent the entire past twelve hours staring at the ceiling of my bedroom, wondering what the fallout would be after tonight's dinner.

Where would the pieces land? Would he finally be as miserable as me? Would Nora look at me like I was a monster?

Three delicious courses had already been served, and we were waiting for dessert to make its way out from the kitchen. The candles, dozens of them lining the table and surfaces around the room, twinkled off of the mirrored dining room walls.

I place my napkin down and survey the table, finally ready to break Bennett McAlister. My conscience struggles, tearing in two. On one side, my vendetta against her stepfather keeps me grounded. But on the other, Nora's small, warm hand is placed on my leg under the table. Her fingers flirt innocently with the fabric of my pants; I don't even think she's aware that her thumb is stroking back and forth.

In my kamikaze mission to take them all down, I didn't realize I'd actually fall for her. For this firecracker genius of an American, with her blunt ways and innocent assumptions of the world. Last night had been our final happy moment together, not that she had realized it. She'd thought it had brought us closer together, that I was a permanent object in her life that she would always be able to count on.

That was all about to come crashing down.

"You don't recognize me, do you?" I stare at Bennett, my nerves cooler than ice water.

He laughs a little, and Nora squeezes my leg. "Only so much as I've seen you around my house, mate."

I don't smile. "I don't look like anyone to you, maybe someone you knew in your past. Take a hard look."

His eyes roam over my face, not catching anything that he sees familiar. "I'm confused ..."

"Asher, what is this about?" Nora's voice is friendly but nervous.

"I thought you would have seen her in me somewhere. You do remember Jane, don't you?"

Her name seems to spark him, and I see the color drain from his features. White hot vengeance circles in my stomach, and my heart is singing with evil glee.

"I'm sorry ... I'm not sure what you're talking about." Bennett's eyes are shifty as the two women watch the exchange.

His denial kicks me in the gut. "You're a swine, a privileged pretty boy who took what he wanted and threw it away when he'd used it up!"

Nora's face wears an expression of sheer confusion and raw upset. "Asher ... what are you even talking about!?"

I take a deep breath, trying to collect my thoughts. "Ten years ago, your stepfather was the reason that my mother died. He'd started an affair with a married woman, one who loved him so dearly that she nearly abandoned her infant son and husband to carry on the tryst. You kept her dangling." I turn to the accused now, my words molten lava. "Bringing her close, making her promises, and then cutting her off because you knew the bloody royals would turn on you if they ever knew what you'd been doing. You ruined her, turned her into a desperate, shell of a person. That night you called for her to come, she drank too much, and threatened you. Didn't she?! She wanted to expose your relationship, to run away with you. I know all the details, I've obsessed over my mother's murder for ten years. You told her to get out, that you were ending things and you'd deny it all if she went to the press. You basically put the keys in her hand, made her drive into the pitch black night while she was legless."

Rachel makes a choked, strangled sob, her eyes glued to Bennett as he stares straight at me. Nora is silent, and I can't turn to her because I don't want to see the look on her face.

"What do you think her last thoughts were before she hit the water? When she went over the side of the bridge, do you think she saw my face? Or do you think she was still crying over you breaking her heart?"

Sour spit coats the inside of my mouth, and a giant ulcer-size hole in my stomach burns with the relief of finally getting all of the built up rage out of my system. My bones feel tired, my shoulders sag with cathartic pressure.

"Bennett ... what is he talking about?" Rachel mumbles

through the fist that is raised to her mouth, her teeth making indent marks in the skin.

His head whips to her, and I can see the sweat on his brow. "Rachel ... I, I wasn't a good man back then. I was a different person, with different priorities. I never meant for anyone ... I never meant for her to get hurt."

"I'm going to be sick." She rushes up from the table and flees the room.

Bennett's chair scrapes the floor, but before he can follow her, I'm standing and pointing. "Sit down."

He eyes me as if I'm about to jump across the table and strangle him. "I'm sorry. I'm so sorry ... I never meant for your family to get hurt."

"It's about ten years too late for that. Mourning at her funeral, pretending you didn't know her ... you're the worst kind of man. And you'll only realize what it feels like to have your soul ripped out if the same thing is done to you."

I turn to Nora for the first time since I started to derail this crazy train. Tears slide down her cheeks, and her eyes hold a mix of sympathy for me, and astonishment at the scene that just played out.

"Since you stepped foot on my homeland, I was waiting to meet you. Plotting out how I would approach you, get you to talk to me and eventually fall for me. Every action I've taken, every time I flirted with you or touched your body ... it was all in the hopes that one day I'd be here."

She gasps, and I feel like I'm ripping my own heart out of my chest. Before tonight, I thought my soul had been black with the soot of my mistakes. Now I knew that the color black was a shade I could no longer use in description for it, that I was so past gone there was no word that compared.

I turn to Bennett. "I fucked your stepdaughter, took her innocence. Just like you took mine. Just like you took my mothers.

And now, Rachel will know what a bloody prick you are, how you've tarnished her family."

If there was a word strong enough for the look of betrayal written all over Nora's face, I'd use it now. My heart felt like a ground up piece of meat, and my head ached like someone was slamming a brick against it. I'd done it, finally come into Bennett's life and mucked it all up like he'd done mine.

Job done, I turned on my heel and began to walk out of the room.

But his voice stops me. "I'm sorry. I'm more sorry than you'll ever know. I should have come to you and your father when she died, I should have stopped it long before that. I should have been a better man. You will never know how truly sorry I am for all of it. But ... I do know that you may have just ruined all of my happiness, and I'm the one who feels sorry for you. Because your mother would have wanted better than this for you. She adored you, she revered you. Jane would never have wanted you to hold this rage and coldness."

I don't turn around, I just feel the daggers of his words cut deep into the flesh of my back.

It should feel like an epiphany in my muscles, a surge in my system. Completing my mission, avenging my mother ... I'd always imagined it would be glorious.

But, as difficult as it is to admit it, Bennett is right. The victory feels empty, spiritless.

I'm left with nothing but a heavy heart and a confused conscience.

Three Months Later

With all of the research and knowledge I have digested about science and biology, I still do not understand how human emotion factors into our makeup.

Sure, I understand studies like anthropology and sociology and psychology, that we react to certain pheromones and we have triggers in our brains that unlock anger or humor or even love.

But I still don't grasp why we can't just turn these off. Why we can't listen to reason and just stop being sad or mad or even stop yearning for a certain person. Whatever the reason may be why we can't, I wish I could solve it. I wish I could erase memories and hours of my life, go back before it hurt so much.

An errant tear breaks away, as it seems to all the time now, and I wipe it before I can start bawling again. Even after twelve weeks, you would think I'd be able to shut it all off, just move on and forget about it. But even now, as May closed in, I couldn't seem to get over it. The crack of betrayal that oozed hurt and pain in the middle of my heart was nowhere near healed. Every night I lie awake, thinking about what he'd said over and over and over again.

Thinking about the look in his eyes when he'd thrown me aside like a stray dog, kicking me before he left me out in the proverbial rain. Or how, just days before, I'd given him the most valuable thing I'd ever have to give. And he took it, breaching my trust and making my world flip on a dime. I wasn't the same girl I had been when we'd landed in London, and now I was even further from that girl.

"Are you crying again?" A soothing voice hits my ears, but I keep my gaze out the window.

In the garden outside, the plants and flowers are blooming, coming out of the long, lonely winter we all had. It should bring hope, but I don't feel the cloud of gloom clear up from over my head.

Swiping at my cheeks, where tears I hadn't even realized had fallen rolled, I nod. "I can't help it, I'm sorry."

"Baby girl, don't you ever apologize for nursing your broken heart. It's a part of life we all have to go through. You work through it in whatever way you feel is best." Mom's strong arms wrap around me as she sits on the arm of the plush chair I'm curled up in.

"But he doesn't deserve it." My voice cracks.

"They hardly ever do." Her tone is far off, and I know she's not thinking about Asher Frederick the way I am.

The past three months have been exceedingly hard on her. After that fateful dinner, she was appalled with Bennett. Hurt that he'd never told her about Jane, gobsmacked that she was living with someone who had broken up a family. For two days after Asher had dropped the atomic bomb, she'd stayed in a guest room in our palace residence, refusing to see Bennett until she could collect her thoughts. I didn't want to see him either, but I was like a child caught in the middle of divorce. Those two days were like the Cold War in our house, harsh ice covered every interaction. Bennett looked haggard, like his heart had been torn out of his chest and he was slowly dying from not being able to look at my mother. He'd slept outside of her door, his bones rattling every time he got up off the hardwood.

It just so happened that some of the greatest news of my life came in those two days, the fat envelope from the University of Pennsylvania overshadowed by the drama playing out in our home. After two days, Mom emerged from the guest room and stated that she and I were going home for a college tour, and that we'd be back in a week. Bennett begged her to let him come, apologizing up and down, but she'd told him she needed this time away. He respected it, and let her go. Watching him, I knew it had taken all of the strength inside of him to let the most precious thing in his life just walk away, not knowing if she'd come back.

Throughout the flights, and the trip, the sorrow was palpable on both of our flesh. What had happened, how our hearts had broken, it wasn't something we were going to get over anytime soon. That night would play on in my head for years to come.

I pushed the thoughts aside, though, as we'd returned home, never feeling more grateful than I was in that moment. The cobwebs of homesickness were finally shaken off my bones, and realizing that what I'd worked so hard for was finally paying off was a big sense of pride that soothed my aching soul.

On the plane back to London, Mom had turned to me.

"Do you think I should forgive Bennett?"

Just thinking about why she needed to forgive him made me cringe. I'd brought this upon them, I'd allowed Asher to breach our security and happiness. I'd fallen for his lies, and now everyone was paying the price.

I wasn't happy with my soon-to-be stepfather, but I'd seen how this was tearing him apart. "Do you think you should?"

She chuckled lightly. "You've always been my mirror, showing me the things I'd rather not face but doing it all the same."

I considered her sentence. "Mom, I know that you love me, that you'd do anything for me … but was there ever a time in your life that you thought everything would be easier if you hadn't had a child so young?"

Her red hair swings angrily over her shoulder as she squarely faces me. "Nora, don't ever say anything like that. You're my child and there is not one day I've ever wished for that."

"Mom, I'm not saying it to upset you, or because I feel that way. I've never felt like you didn't want me. But … you know me, I look at things logically. Even if you say you never wished that, a part of you deep down must have felt it. When you were working a double shift at the diner, or paying for clothes that I'd ripped unnecessarily. I think … I think right now it's the same way with Bennett. Ten years ago, he made mistakes. Terrible mistakes. But … you haven't even heard his side yet. You aren't giving him any benefit of the doubt, and I know that beyond everything, you love him more than you can say. You wouldn't have uprooted your life for just anyone. The Bennett you know could be a completely different man than the one Asher described."

It was like a knife slicing each ventricle of my heart to say his name.

Her smile is a proud one. "How did I ever get blessed with such a wise daughter? You always awe me, my girl. You're going to do amazing things … you already do."

I shrug. "I just believe that most people deserve a second chance."

"After everything that boy said and did to you, for you to still *believe that is such a miracle. And I believe it too. I believe that even the most damaged of us deserves a second chance."*

What Asher had done to my family hadn't taught me that though. I had learned that some people were worth fighting for, worth saving. And that others were more damned than we could ever imagine. Asher had educated me, but not in the way he'd planned. He had sought to tear apart my family, to ruin Bennett and send my mom running. But when you knew what real, genuine love felt like, that could prevail over anything.

Three months later, we were all stronger than ever in our relationships with each other. Bennett had sat down with each of us, telling us the truth of what had happened with Jane. How he'd messed up, and then tried to break it off only for her to not be able to let it go. He had cared for her, but eventually the truth of what he was doing to her son and husband made him sick. That night, she'd come over in a panic and he'd tried to stop her, but she ran out. And what Asher was so broken over happened, and no one could ever take it back.

"How was your therapy session?" I looked up into her eyes, which were clear and sure.

My mom, the rock of my life. "It was actually very good. We talked about the wedding more, and I feel like we are moving past it. Thank you, honey, for urging me to be a bigger person. You make me a better person every day, you know that? Sometimes I think you're the adult."

It had been easy to be honest, to encourage her to make things right with Bennett. I wanted them to get married, I wanted my mom happy. And if therapy was a good road to that, then I was all for it.

"So how are things looking for the wedding? When is your next dress fitting?" I try to move us onto a happier topic.

The wedding was only a month away, and the whole country was abuzz with excitement.

"Next weekend, and they have your dress ready too." She clapped her hands, and I could not wait to see both of them.

The designer was basically a living legend, and our fairy tale seemed picture perfect whenever we were in his studio.

Mom talks about a few other decisions they've made, but my mind is trapped in its perpetual thought process, over analyzing and worrying. I've had an anxiety attack almost weekly, and for the first time in my life, I don't want to go to school.

Besides my mom marrying Bennett, I can't wait to fly to UPenn in August and leave all of this behind.

One of the only positives of this whole fiasco has been that we've gotten to deal with it in private. No press, no paps. I can't imagine the shit storm that would fly if Bennett's mistake ten years ago was made public.

A glass shatters on the side of the wall, and I don't even cringe. Shoes crunch over the broken shards, curses muttered as he rounds the corner.

"Why hasn't anything gone public yet?! It's been three bloody months, and he's still sitting in his goddamn throne room, getting his knob polished by his little American slag!" My father roars, his face redder than I've ever seen it.

Because Rachel and Nora Randolph are better people than you'll ever be, and even if they are devastated, they would never leak anything personal about their family or Bennett to the press.

He's losing it, and I'm just fading deeper into my despair. From the moment that news broke that the American peasants turned princesses would be moving to London, it was a marathon to the finish line for me. I bided my time, grew close to Nora, gained her trust, worked my way into her body, and then crushed them all like ants under my boot.

Except, I hadn't accounted for the feelings I would gain for her. How interwoven my emotions would be with the girl that I made my mission ... how dark and steep my slide into oblivion would be.

Nora was, for all intents and purposes, the one shining spot I would ever have in my life. Her laugh, the way she looked at me as if I was just as innocent and pure as her, all of the things we'd done together. They were all gone, I'd robbed us of all of our light.

And so far, the only person it had seemed to hurt was me. Sure, there was speculation when Nora and her mother went home to visit the American college she'd been accepted to, just another thing I wasn't around for. But they'd come back, were photographed with Bennett, seeming to still be the perfect family unit they'd been since before the dinner from hell.

"I'm going to have to leak it to the press then. Bloody hell, I always thought by exposing him to the ones he loved the most, that they'd do the hard part for me. But I underestimated the callousness of those two peasants."

My father picks up his cellphone, his shirt collar wrinkled and his hair out of place. He'd never looked more desperate, and I was suddenly fearful.

Leaping out of the chair I'm sitting in, I try to grab his phone. "No! You're not going to leak this."

For three months, I'd watched him become unhinged. He wasn't proud of me, the way I'd always envisioned. It hadn't brought him closure, only further toward the brink of insanity. I hadn't realized until just recently that there was no way to please him, to make him happy in this lifetime. Too much damage had been done, and he wasn't the type of person to let it go.

But I wasn't about to let him take me, or Nora and her family, down with him.

"What are you doing, you twit! Give that to me, *now*. I'm going to correct what you clearly couldn't accomplish. Christ, never leave a little boy to do a man's job."

His words stung, like cigarette burns to my skin. I'd lived under his influence for so long, fed the same bullshit day by day.

And in the end, it hadn't made anything better. It only proved that he would never love or care for me the way I wished he could, and that I needed to get out from under him. I needed to be free.

"If you leak this, I'll go to the press." I stand tall, my shoulders squaring for a fight.

He cackled, the sound hollow and malicious. "And say what, you tosser? Tell them how useless you are?"

Inside, my heart cracked further open. "No, I will tell them what you assigned me to do to Nora and her family. I'll tell them all the sordid details, and describe what it is you've done to others in our community. You forget that I'm a good listener, father ... I know things that you don't want any other person to know. Your reputation will be tarnished ... but even worse in your eyes, the Frederick name will be tarnished. You'll be the laughing stock of London, and none of these blithering idiots you call friends will ever speak to you again. So go ahead, muck up Bennett McAlister's life. But just know that if you do, you're going down with him."

My father's face was the shade of burning coals, dark and ruddy. "You spineless little shit! You've ruined everything! You're a disgrace."

A renewed sense of strength courses through me. "You know what, coming from you, that is a compliment. I'm glad I've disgraced and disappointed you, because I never should have wanted to impress you in the first place. You're evil, a prick with a hard on for revenge and eyes for nothing else. My mother would be ashamed, in me and for what I've done."

"You know nothing about your mother." His voice is somber.

"And neither do you. There are two sides to every story, *Dad*. Why did she cheat? What was happening here that she felt she needed to leave us? I may not remember many things about her, but I do know that it wasn't all of her fault. And it wasn't all

Bennett's. I'm done listening to your delusions, and I'm done being your errand boy."

His fists grow white with how hard he's clenching them. "You have no idea what it's like to be on your own. I've given you everything, *everything* a person could want."

I knew he would throw that wrench into it. "You can't touch me, and my trust fund is mine. A gift from Mum and her family, if you didn't forget. And you may have given me money, but you never gave me what a parent should."

My whole life, I'd been made to feel as if I was a nuisance, or an afterthought. He hadn't come to my achievements, been present for birthdays or milestones. Money might make the world go around, but I was beginning to realize that there was nothing that came close to being loved and cared for. And while I may never feel it like the way I had with Nora, I wasn't going to settle anymore. I wasn't going to live in this dark place with him.

Without another word, I turned on my heel and stormed out of our townhouse and onto Downing Street. The sidewalk was thin with pedestrians, almost everyone already at home eating supper with their families.

Leaving another person behind in my life should have made the hole in my gut grow wider. But ... it didn't. The weight was finally lifted, the expectations and pressure and false realities taken off of my shoulders.

I didn't have a clue where to go from here, or how to do anything when I'd been brought up in a world where every single thing was taken care of for me. But I'd figure it out. It was about time.

And I was ready.

"**M**ate, just go talk to her." Drake unwraps the protein bar he's holding and chomps off a bite.

I stare down and across the hall, catching a glimpse of burnt orange hair buried in her locker.

None of my friends know what happened, but they know that all communication between Nora and I has stopped.

"I can't, it won't make any difference. Just drop it." I place my textbooks in my locker, eager for this school year to be over.

Not that I know fully what I'm doing next year. Sure, I still have my Oxford acceptance, and I could attend and be privy to the same college experience every Frederick has gotten for generations. I could continue to live the cushy life that's been provided, and stay close to London.

But, I was trying something new. Or at least I was struggling to. Opening my trust fund was never something I thought I would have to do. The large nest egg of money was going to be gone eventually, sometime in the distant future, and then I'd be on my own. It was both terrifying and exhilarating.

"Fine, just hate to see my girl so upset. She won't even joke around with me anymore." I had noticed that she wasn't really speaking to any one in our group anymore, save for Eloise. "So when do I get to see your bachelor pad? I can't believe you went out and bought a bloody flat!"

My flat was nothing to brag about, a small one bedroom in the quiet neighborhood of Chelsea. It was clean, updated with nice furnishings, and best of all ... it was all mine. I'd used a sizable portion of my trust fund on it, but at least I knew I would always have a home in the city I'd grown up in if it came to it.

"Soon ... maybe. I'm actually enjoying being alone, and I don't need you wankers coming in and mucking the place up."

"Alone? Come on, don't tell me you haven't had some fit birds coming over to your solo place, shagging 'em like crazy?!" His eyes speak volumes, telling me I must be crazy.

"You wouldn't get it." I close my locker, the bell ringing and the hallways emptying out.

"Jeez, mate, sorry. I get it, I'm proud of you ... I know your dad isn't the easiest of guys."

His eyes speak something else, and I wonder if my friends know more than they let on about my home life.

Glancing down the hall, I see that Nora is dragging behind everyone. "I'll catch you later, mate."

I don't wait for his goodbye, but instead start quickly toward her. In the months since that dinner, I've seen her at school almost every day. At first I acted cold, wanting my message from the dinner to sink in. I wanted them to hurt ... but those feelings vanished very quickly. About five days after I'd spewed all of that hate in their home, I came face to face with Nora in the hall.

And in her eyes, I'd seen all of the damage I'd done. The hurt, the rejection, the betrayal. That look she gave me spoke louder than words ever could have, and I felt repulsive.

I didn't expect her to ever talk to me, let alone look at me, again ... but I had to try. I couldn't continue to sit in this despair, and even if she never accepted my apology, I had to make it.

The hall was empty, and she seemed to be engrossed in something in her locker.

"Hi." Smooth opening, Asher.

She looks up slowly, knowing my voice. Her eyes don't shine like they used to, at least not for me. She doesn't talk, but shuts her locker and turns like she might bolt.

I step in front of her. "Please, Nora ... let me explain."

My tone is desperate, and maybe that sparks something inside of her. "I don't know what more you could possibly say to me."

"You don't ... there is so much more to it all. Could we just talk somewhere?" I wanted so badly to just reach out and touch her.

I ached for her when I was alone, and pretty much all the time. I missed her conversation, her odd observations, even her shy naïveté. I missed the words she used, so complicated and sophisticated that I couldn't do anything but laugh. I missed the way she chewed on the end of a pen when she studied, how her hair fell into her face every time she laughed, the aimless conversations we had over coffee for her and tea for me. But when I was here, standing in front of her, the ache grew into a massive throb of need. I'd wasted so much time, spent hours and minutes plotting against her when I should have been caring for her. We had only gotten the one time in my room, and I needed more.

She tilted her head, taking my request in. "What reasons could you ever have for trying to break apart my family? To ruin my stepfather? For so long, *so long* Asher, you lied to me. You made me trust you. I don't ... I don't even know what good excuse you could make to explain that."

She was right of course, but I pleaded still. "Please, you don't know what it was like. The home I grew up in, the propaganda I was fed."

"I may not, but you chose to do what you did. Chose to pursue me, to sleep with me! Do you know that before you, I hadn't opened myself up to anyone like that. And thanks to you, I probably won't again. You're a bad person, Asher, and how you grew up might have influenced it, but it doesn't change how you truly are inside."

Her words slice me, making the bleeding gash in my soul even wider. I nod, accepting that she will never allow me to explain. There is that cliché saying that if you love something, you must let it go. And as stereotypical as it was, Nora had taught me to love through a time where I should have been staying far away from her.

And now it was my turn to suffer. To let her despise me and never look my way again. It was my penance; the cross I had hung around my neck and was now forced to bear.

For her, I would do it. Just as on the first day of the school year, one of us turns on a heel and walks away from the other. But this time, it's me.

There is exactly one month until my high school graduation, and it cannot come fast enough.

When I'd lived in Pennsylvania, I couldn't wait to get out. I'd daydream about grabbing my diploma on the school football field and sprinting for the closest bus station or airport. But now ... I couldn't wait to go home. To land my two feet on some Philadelphia soil and breathe in that polluted air that everyone in London makes fun of.

It's been a ball exploring Europe, but *they*, whoever they are, weren't lying when they said there is no place like home. I know I will come back here, but the last three hundred days or so have been a whirlwind, and I need a break.

There is also the tricky matter of seeing Asher and all of his friends every single day, even though for the most part, they've forgotten about me. Only Eloise has kept in touch, because I actually make the effort to talk to her.

"So the royal wedding is coming, yeah? Must be fucking brilliant to have the best of the best waiting on you hand and foot. I hear Mendoza is designing your mother's dress ... is it bloody amazing?"

I smile, not letting anything slip. "You know I can't deny or confirm any of that, Eloise."

She points a salad-clad fork at me, our table in the corner of the lunchroom kind of out of the way of the popular crowd that congregated in the middle. "And here I thought we were mates."

For some reason, she still kept trying to get me to open up to her, even if I wasn't going on the group's international party trips or sneaking into closets at royal functions. Maybe she wanted the inside information, but I tried not to let what Asher did to me cloud my judgment. I chose to believe that since she'd come from a similar background, she commiserated with my position. And maybe it was a little easier hanging out with someone cut from the same cloth.

I watch her, the diamond studs in her ears sparkling. Around the room, girls and boys lean the most expensive leather bags against chairs on the ground, their Rolex watches and Cartier jewelry gleaming. Shoes the price of a small country are laced on their feet, the meals they consume some of the finest food in the world ... not to mention that of a high school cafeteria.

Me? I'm still rocking the plain Winston uniform, pearl studs from Forever 21 in my ears. My nails are bare, the cuticles shredded from where I've been biting them. Almost a year in this world, and it really hadn't jaded me as I'd feared, and some had hoped, it would. In part, I had to thank Asher. He'd shown me just how cruel and harsh this world could be, just like he'd promised he would at the beginning, and I'd grown from his betrayal. Now I was ready to go back to the real world.

"We are, which is why I will save you a dance with me at the wedding." I planned on letting loose after the ceremony.

With all of the pent-up stress and double the paparazzi following us around at all times, I was ready for the day to be here. I think Mom was too, but that was mostly because she just couldn't wait to be married to Bennett. It was truly inspiring the way they'd forged together after that dinner with Asher. It was also why I could remain mostly positive about being vulnerable and opening up more to people. Sure, there were bad people out there, but there were also people worth showing your true self to. And I was holding out for those people.

"Christ, I love weddings. Free booze, dancing, single men ... what more could you ask for? You can bet I'm going to find the most eligible bachelor. Unless you want him, of course. It's your home court, so you get advantage."

I gulp as I look down at my plate of sushi. The hardest part of losing my virginity and all of the aftermath was not being able to talk about it with anyone. I couldn't talk to my mom about such things; not because she wouldn't listen supportively but because it was all just too awkward. I didn't want to talk to Eloise about having sex for the first time, because I didn't trust that she wouldn't laugh about it. And I also couldn't divulge the details of Asher and I's break up, because if any of that information ever got out my family would be ruined.

Suffering in silence is making this ten times harder, but I shut my trap. "They're all for you, girl. I'll be so busy running around making sure things are perfect, I won't have time to ogle."

She picks at a bright purple cuticle and smirks. "Not that you want to. It's okay to admit that you're still hung up on Frederick."

I roll my eyes, playing it off. "It's been months, Eloise ... I'm over it. And I'm sure he is too."

Her laugh is sardonic and teasing. "Oh, yeah right, that's why he tracks you with his eyes every hour of the school day like some lovesick puppy."

"He does?" It pops out of my mouth before I can stop it.

I shouldn't care, should be able to biologically cut off the feeling. But I can't. I still lie awake, thinking about the night that we'd connected so intensely that my whole body still flushed just recalling it. I'd never known how it would feel, how in-tune your body and your partner's body could become.

She quirks an eyebrow. "Like you're the poshest thing since tea time."

There shouldn't be a niggle of satisfaction that tingles in my heart, but there is.

"So, one month, huh? What's your plan?" I change the subject.

She shrugs, picking at the ingredients in her salad. "The Sorbonne, so I can educate people on why food like this is terrible."

Surprise lights my face. "Really? I didn't know you were into cooking ..."

Eloise smiles. "There are a lot of things this group doesn't know about me, Nora. See, when you're trying to be cool and part of the in-crowd, you hide the interesting and unique tidbits about yourself. But after Winston, I just get to be me. I get to leave here and pursue my dreams. Not everyone is eager to stay ... some of us are like you, and can't wait to get out."

I realize that in all of the time I've spent with her, I haven't genuinely tried to get to know her. And that's sad. "I apologize, really. I should have asked sooner, or at least had you cook me a meal."

"We still have some time. I'll make you one of my signature dishes, and you can bring your Netflix and we can binge watch Friends. I do love me some American TV."

I laugh, because it's just so her. "Well, you'll have to come visit me in Philadelphia next year then. I'll get you a proper cheesesteak and we'll go to a football game."

"American football or soccer? Because you Americans are so wonky with that."

"American football, baby ... with the pads and tight pants and men tackling each other over a ball."

She snorts. "It's the same in our kind of football dear, but bugger if I don't love the sport for that."

"Have you ever been to the States?" The British endearment for it feels funny coming off my lips.

"I've been to New York and Los Angeles of course, but I haven't done the whole suburban States tour. You'll have to take me. I'll wear jean shorts and flip-flops, and drink out of plastic cups from whatever that store is you've mentioned before."

"Wawa? Ha! I'd love to see you filling a Slurpee cup, it would be so domestic of you."

"And maybe you'll introduce me to a cowboy, one with real boots."

I roll my eyes. "Eloise, I'm from Pennsylvania, not the deep south of Texas. While we have farms, they don't typically house the kind of stereotype you're looking for."

"Whatever. Just know that I'm driving your car on the wrong side of the road when I visit."

Just thinking about that made me laugh. A bittersweet kind of chuckle, because while I was ready to get to college, and back to people on the same level as myself, I was also going to miss the few connections I'd made here.

31

Having no true family, and a very small circle of people that I knew continuously while growing up, I've actually never attended a wedding before. So planning for my mother's big day, while a challenge, was also kind of fun.

Pinteresting and prepping, picking out colors and dresses and centerpieces and fun personal artifacts to include in the decor ... it had been a labor of love for us both. I'd seen the odd romantic comedy wedding, even watched that silly show about picking your wedding dress. I knew that some people went over the top, and that the entire industry was just a money-making machine.

But I had absolutely no clue just how out-of-this-world her wedding day would actually be.

"This is insane." I smile through my teeth as Mom looks adoringly at the crowd.

And when I say crowd, I mean ... literally every person who has ever resided in London. Women cheering and crying, wearing shirts with Mom and Bennett's faces on them. Little kids running around with flowers, tossing them at the glass top car we're sitting in. Men yelling about how they love my mother, and God Save the Queen. So many faces line the street, everyone clamoring for a glance at the beautiful bride.

"Just smile and wave." Mom doesn't look rattled in the least, her hands sitting calmly in her lap.

I can't help but smile, feeling the infectious glow from her. All day, she's been nothing but relaxed and joyful. Through the makeup and hair, to getting into her dress fit for a real live queen, to pictures on the grounds before we left … she never once complained of nerves or agitation. Whatever worries were there, whatever last minute details to plan, it all vanished. She was going to meet Bennett at the church, and I could tell that to her, that was all that mattered.

"Are you nervous?" I ask her for the fifth time, not able to hold it back because I'm a little shaky.

She reaches across the seat, and grasps my hand. "I'm not at all, honey. But it's understandable if you are. It's a big step, one that seals our life. But it doesn't mean we stop being us, it will always be me and you against the world. We just … are adding Bennett too. And the three of us, we're going to support and love each other no matter what. I promise."

Her eyes are glassy with unshed tears, and I swallow down the lump in my throat that has formed. "I love you, Mom."

We watch as the people blur, the long road to the church filled with loudness. When we finally pull up, the cream carpet rolled all the way to where we got out of the car door, my butter-flies are at an all-time high. The noise outside the car is deafen-ing, and people chant my mom's name.

She gets out first, her exit graceful and noble in every action. Her hand cups, waving to the crowd like the queen-to-be she's about to become. The megawatt smile on her face is not for show, I know it because I feel every ounce of her happiness in my bones as well.

I get out, my long light purple dress blowing in the soft spring air. Mom let me choose my dress, a tulle creation with a lace on the upper part and thick straps that lifted my boobs a little higher than they actually were. It fit me in all the right places, but was still so beautiful and just ... lovely.

The crowd roars again, and I wave sheepishly. I'm not used to all of this, have forgotten the training as if my head was on fire each time I get out in front of people. I wasn't bred for it, and it's not super important that I learn all of the aspects as I'm leaving for college in the fall. I won't be subjected to as much scrutiny or public outings ... but I know how to behave when it's needed of me.

"*Beautiful!*"

"*Radiant!*"

"*Brilliant!*"

The sidewalks gush with compliments, praise ringing out from every corner. Silently, I thank the heavens that no one is throwing any insults or questions at her. Walking over to her, I squeeze her hand before moving behind her and picking up the train of her dress. The lace is like butter beneath my fingertips, and I choke up at just how beautiful she looks.

"You ready?" I ask over the noise.

Mom turns around, her veil now put down over her face. "I have never been more ready in my life."

Together, we start for the church, the doors opening to the sound of organ music. My heart soars and flies, the overwhelmingness of it all too much. Tears form at the corners of my eyes, this moment such a long haul for Mom and Bennett. They deserved today.

Everyone stood in the church, the high painted ceilings looking down on us with their angels and gods. White marble and gray slate make up the incredible arches and statues, crucifixes and stained glass making the whole building feel otherworldly. The pews were packed, but Mom's head never swiveled from the straight on view she had toward the end of the aisle.

Bennett stands at the end in his British military uniform, his medals and patches hanging brilliantly from the lapels and shoulders. I always imagine princes and kings being stoic on momentous occasions, but my stepfather, he wears his emotions on his sleeve. Maybe it's why the public loves him so much.

He only has eyes for Mom, his smile so wide it could rival the width of Texas. He waits impatiently, twisting his fingers and jiggling his feet. The walk is long but builds the anticipation, everyone adoringly looking on at Mom and I. I make sure her train isn't twisting, that she can walk correctly, that everything in this moment is so perfect that even the Hallmark Channel couldn't do it better.

Finally, we get to the altar, Bennett helping Mom climb the steps to join him. I smooth out her dress and then move to my reserved seat in the first pew.

And I watch, we all watch, as a fairytale unfolds literally before our eyes. As two people are joined in the most binding way possible on this earth. As they vow to trust and protect and love each other, to serve out their duties in unison.

Tears fall down my cheeks, a mixture of happiness and sadness. Happy at a new chapter blooming, at my Mom getting the one thing she'd always wanted, at becoming a family with an honorable man like Bennett. But sorrow creeps in, Asher's face in my mind and the days of it just being Mom and I now vanishing.

Simpler times are over, and this is our reality. It may be a privileged, beautiful one, but I know it will complicated and flawed.

S hock wracks my body, my fingers trying to snap together. I can't feel them, can't hear anything over the ringing in my ears.

I can't believe what had just happened, my senses dulled but so sharp at the same time. Was this what they meant about people being able to act quickly in a crisis?

My lilac dress was torn at the hem around my feet where David Frederick had grabbed at it. Asher's lip was bleeding, but he stood like an intimidating warrior over his father's crumpled form. The last twenty minutes were a blur; David sitting in the corner of the room that held our purses, accusing me of things I'd never done, arguing with me, threatening me ... and then lunging.

And then, he'd been gone even as I'd crouched, trying to avoid the blow he'd surely land.

"Don't you dare touch her, ever!" he growls, his eyes are a scary shade of dark green.

"Nora!" My mother rushes in, the train of her wedding dress trailing behind her.

Bennett follows, a security guard tailing them both. They're the royal crown prince and princess now, that deal was sealed just minutes ago. Their detail will be heightened, something I'm very glad for in this moment.

My stepfather takes one glance at the scene, and begins to act. He points to David and addresses the guard. "Get backup and take this man out of here at once. Detain him. And bring a medical kit."

The guard starts out of the room, and Mom rushes to me. "Are you okay? Oh my God …"

Sheer terror marks her face, and instantly I feel guilty for bringing this drama into her life. "I'm fine, I'm okay. Asher … he got here in time."

They both turn to Asher, who is still monitoring his father like he might get up and try something again.

Bennett moves to him, touching his arm like he's trying to soothe a wild animal. "That's a brilliant job, son. Now come sit down."

Asher looks at him like he might swing at him next, but cautiously lets his guard down, letting Bennett lead him to a chair at the table in the corner.

"He got you pretty good, but I think you got him better." My stepfather dabs at Asher's lip with a napkin, and I can't believe the situation that is unfolding in front of me.

My system is still in overdrive from almost being attacked, my heart pounding and hands shaking. Mom holds me, watching the two men interact. After all of it, what Bennett did ten years ago, how it affected Asher, what he tried to do to our family, him saving me just seconds ago … my stepfather was still the good man I knew he could be.

And Asher … to say I was surprised would be an extreme under-statement. Everything comes rushing at me. What Eloise said about his family, the way he'd begged me in the hallway at Winston to just let him explain. It didn't forgive what he'd done or how he'd lashed out at that dinner, but seeing the way his father had just advanced at me, it gave a glimpse inside what life must have been like for him.

"I'm sorry ... I told him not to try anything today." Asher buries his face in his hands.

"You don't have anything to apologize for." Bennett rubs his shoulder.

Someone comes in with the first aid kit, and Mom takes it from them. "Let me take a look at that lip."

She tends to Asher, and I still can't make my feet move. After she dabs some ointment and places a Band-Aid over the cut, those green eyes latch onto me.

"I didn't know he would ... I never meant for this to happen." His expression pleads with me again.

It's then that I'm unlocked from my body's prison, my feet moving to join them all over by the table. I kneel down, showing him that I'm okay.

"Thank you for being here, he didn't hurt me." I touch my hand to his.

That familiar electricity comes zapping back, and I want him to wrap me up in those big arms right here. But I hold back, confused and still shaken.

"Can I have a few minutes alone with Asher?" Bennett looks at Mom and me.

"No, it's your wedding day, I should go ..." He protests, getting up and trying to leave.

Mom lays a hand on his shoulder. "We're already married, and we have a lifetime together. Stay, you should hear what he has to say. Come on, sweetheart, you can help me bustle my train."

She takes a hold of my hand. I give Asher one last look, trying to convey all of the feelings swirling around my system.

He nods, and I know we haven't seen the last of each other today.

Mom leads me into another room in the basement of the church. "Are you really okay, baby?"

Her hands search my face, and I shake her off. "I'm sure, just a little frazzled is all. I didn't notice him in the room until he started talking ... Mom, he was delirious. Spouting off about how I'd ruined his life, and if it weren't for me he would be king right now. He sounded ... crazy."

She nodded, her face so flawless and beautiful on this day. "He was, honey. Something must have snapped; some things drive people to drastic measures. I'm just glad that Asher was there, what that boy did for you was very brave. And standing up to his father, it's not an easy task I'd bet."

Her words were meant to get me thinking, and they did. Under all of the layers I'd already seen, maybe there was more to Asher Frederick than I'd ever imagined.

33

There is no description for the exhaustion my body feels in this moment.

This morning, I watched my father fall deeper and deeper into a state of hysteria. Mumbling about becoming king and taking down Nora and Rachel once and for all. He was pacing the halls when I went in, an emergency call by the housekeeper rousing me from my sleep in my Chelsea apartment. I tried to talk some sense into him, even slapped him hard but he just kept going. I'd never seen him this unraveled, and when I went to go talk to the housekeeper, he'd bolted.

I knew from the second I heard the car engine where he was heading. It had taken me thirty minutes to fight my way through the crowds and traffic, parking in a neighborhood behind the church and scaling a wall to get in. Adrenaline had poured through my system, and I'd gone through a utility door in the back of the building to get in. My mission had been to locate Nora, and when I had, all I had to do was watch for my father.

She looked so bloody gorgeous in her bridesmaid dress, the lilac soft against her creamy skin. Everyone standing up on that altar looked so happy, jubilant and blissful to be there in that moment.

I'd watched him follow her into the little rectory room afterwards, heard his threats as she tried to make an escape for the door. I hadn't hesitated.

And now, my lip was bandaged up and I was sitting in this room, trying to make out the ghosts whispering in my ear. There was something wrong with my father, maybe there always had been. His desperation had almost cost me everything. Because even if I couldn't be with her, I realized in that moment when I lunged for my only blood relative still in my life that I loved Nora Randolph more than anyone else on this earth.

"Are you okay?" A tiny voice came from the doorway.

My head whips around and I can't help but stand. "Nora ..."

"No sit." She moves across the room, sitting in the chair beside me.

I reach for her hand, unable to not touch her. "I'm so sorry, so bloody sorry. I didn't know that he would do something like that."

"Like Bennett said, don't apologize. Just ... thank you, for being here."

I looked down at our joined hands, unable to stare into her gorgeous face. "If he had hurt you, I don't know what I would have done. I could never ... Nora, I've missed you every single day. I was so wrong, so wrong."

Her tears glistened when I looked up into those hazel pools. "I have tried to forget you. For so many months all I've wanted to do is forget anything that ever happened between us."

I feel the pain and anguish rolling off her body in waves. "If I could do that for you, I would. If I could go back, do it all over, stop myself ... I would. I would do anything. But I can't. So all I can do is say how bloody sorry I am, and hope that you can forgive me. Because Nora, all I care about is you. I have been such a tosser for so long, fueled by the lies and manipulations of my father. I was buried so deep in them that I couldn't see straight."

She nods. "I know, I understand now. The hate he spewed Asher, I've never seen anyone that desperate or angry."

I feel my way up her arms, needing her velvet skin to soothe me. "Bennett told me the whole story, or at least how he viewed it. My mother ... she felt trapped. She loved me, but my father had been much the same back then as he was now. She couldn't stand to live with him any longer, but knew that if she tried to take a Frederick baby away from the flock, there would be hell to pay. And he couldn't stand to tear her apart like he had for so long. He loved her, but he knew she was suffering. So he ended it, but it only made things worse. My mother had lost the only thing that was keeping her going, that could keep her sane in the house of David Frederick. My father controlled everything, even her interaction with me. So she flew off the handle. Making plans and schemes and trying to get Bennett to run away with her and I. The night that ... she died, he had been trying to stop her from driving. She scratched him so badly in the face that he bled, and before he could do anything about it, her car was already out on that bridge."

My voice cracks thinking about how alone my mother must have felt. How abused by my father she must have been.

"I should have let you explain ..." Nora sounds helpless.

"You owe me nothing. Not after what I did. It's no excuse, but in some ways, I was as trapped as my mother. You saw him, how harsh and brutal he can be. It's all I've ever known. And when the one person you trust tells you over and over again how evil someone is, how they must be destroyed, you believe them. But Nora ... when we were together, nothing I felt with you or said to you was a lie. Beyond all hope, I fell for you. You showed me a side of relationships that I never knew existed. I know you owe me nothing, I know that ... not forgiveness or reciprocation or anything. But ... I'm asking for it anyway. Because I need you. Because I miss you."

My heart aches in my chest, the need to hear her absolve me so strong that I can barely breathe.

"You hurt me ... so badly. Asher, I never ... what I did with you, I had never done that before."

I know she's not just talking about our relationship. She was a virgin, I had my suspicions and still I took that from her. And now she confirmed it.

"There is no amount of I'm sorry in the world. Words don't even do justice to how ashamed of myself I am."

She nods. "I know. I know that. In my brain I can compute that, but my gut ... it still hurts. I've never felt the way I felt about you for anyone else. And to be crushed like that, it's going to take a lot."

I get to my knees, literally begging. "I'm not above making an arse out of myself. Whatever it takes, just give me a chance. You have no reason to say yes, but just one more."

Her expression is apprehensive at best, but I can see the hope gleaming in her eyes. My palms sweat, my face aches from where my father punched me.

"Let's do this. Why don't you come to the reception? I think we could both use a little time to unwind. If after tonight I still feel okay around you, then we can talk."

"Deal." I don't even hesitate, jumping at whatever chance to redeem myself with her that I can.

It's amazing how a little dancing will do the soul some good.

After we arrived at the reception for Mom and Bennett's wedding, I saw Asher in glimpses. Glad that he wasn't hounding me or trying to check on me all night, I got a minute to breathe. To recover a bit from the heaviness of what happened in that rectory at the church.

There wasn't a drink in his hand all night, but we did meet on the dance floor. Our bodies shook in rhythm with the classics that the sixteen-piece band was cranking out. We smiled, even laughed at the goofiness of some of the old fogies trying to bust a move. Mom had insisted on a non-traditional British reception. Instead of a sit-down dinner and drinks in separate men's and women's rooms after, she wanted family style pasta dishes and mini-cheesesteaks passed around during the cocktail hour. She wanted dancing, merriment, and no stuffiness.

Some of the royals and nobles snuffed her for this, deriding her under their breath throughout the night. But we didn't let any of it put a damper on our night. If anything, Mom and

Bennett laughed more because now there was nothing any one could say to them. They were married, and it was a celebration.

At the end of the night, Asher walked me to the car that took the family back to Kensington Palace. We didn't say much, having been all talked out from the hours beforehand. But I'd let him hold me, kiss the crown of my hair. I didn't feel safe in his arms like I used to, but I also didn't feel harmed. I knew, after what his father had done, that his childhood and the trauma he'd been through had tainted his vision of the world, and my family.

Which was why I had agreed to meet him today.

"Hi." I wave cautiously as I near him, eyeing the spread he has laid out.

"Welcome to our picnic." He looks shy, uneasy.

We stand there, neither of us knowing what happens next. I decide to be the bigger person and challenge myself, leaning in for a hug. Mostly, I just can't resist him when he's so close to me, looking so relaxed in his summer shorts and T-shirt.

The hug is warm but fleeting, both of us jumping back into our own personal space before it goes on too long. His arms felt strong, supportive. My heart ached to be close to him again.

"I've never been to this side of the park." I look at the little marble house, surrounded by fountains and gardens. There wasn't much foot traffic here, not like at the Serpentine or the Princess Diana Memorial.

"It's always been one of my favorite parts, not too crowded, like a little Secret Garden." He takes out two sandwiches and a thermos.

"I loved that movie as a little girl. A whole reading garden away from the world with a lock and key? Sign me up."

Asher laughs, a quiet but appreciative laugh. "I could see you loving that. So I got sandwiches from Pret, a crayfish and rocket one for you and a ham and cheese toastie for me. And then I have iced tea, and I brought some of that Milka chocolate that you like."

He hands me my favorite Pret sandwich and the butterflies in my stomach flap their wings. He remembered my order, brought my favorite chocolate ... I should be careful to feel this comfortable with him but the way he's making this semi-date go, I'm weak to his charm.

"Thanks." We eat in silence for a few minutes.

"I know it's not easy for you." He speaks up after he polishes off the last of his sandwich.

"What?" The sun shines down on us, the fragrance of the flowers floating all around us.

"Trusting me. I know it's not easy. I don't know what to say or do to help you get over that ... I know it takes time. I know that I betrayed you, hurt you. I promise on my life, on everything I have, that I will never do that again."

I look down at my hands where they fist in my white sundress. "It's not, honestly. But I realize what you went through wasn't easy either, and I'm going to try. We've resolved what happened, I know that you said things and they were what you thought were accurate. I'm trying to forgive you, but I also can't be mired down in all of the drama any longer. We have to move on from here, a clean slate. There is too much to be happy about to think about that dark time anymore."

And I know that what I say rings true, even in my soul. I don't want to dwell. I'm not going to be as naïve as I was. But I also don't want to hate Asher, or even avoid him. I love him, I know that now, and while I might not tell him ... I also didn't want to fight. I'd seen how love had set my mom free, how happy she and Bennett were. We both had college to look forward to, and with the little time we had, I didn't want to spend any of it dredging up the past.

Asher looks relieved. "That's all I want. Thank you."

"So have you started rowing for the summer yet?" I change the subject on to new things.

He leans back on his elbows, his abs flexing through his shirt. His sunglasses sit low on the bridge of his nose so that I can make out those green eyes. "Yep, summer team has started. But I hate rowing in the summer, it's too hot. Everyone else seems to love the sun and nice weather, but I prefer the cut of the cold. Gives me some sort of edge."

"Oh, you're so hardcore." I roll my eyes.

"Did you like your trip to the college you picked in the States?" When I raise my eyebrow, he explains. "Come on, Nora, you have to know that I was still keeping up with everything you did. You're in the papers all the time, and I missed you."

I can't help the smile that creases my cheeks. "I liked it a lot actually ... it felt good to be back in Pennsylvania. Although Philly is a whole different beast than where I grew up. Have you decided on college? Still Oxford?"

He nods, but I see the hesitation there. "Oxford is still the plan, even though I'm not really following the Frederick path anymore. But I figure, I have to try it out ... it's one of the best schools in the country after all."

"And what's the plan now that you're not sticking to your family's design?"

He shrugs. "I'm not sure to be honest. Rowing, study some kind of business. Be free for the first time in my life. I bought my own flat, if you didn't know."

Surprise works through me. "You did? Where?"

"A little one bedroom in Chelsea. I could have you over sometime, if you want?" He looks like he's trying not to get his hopes up.

"I'd like that." I smile, shyness suddenly coming over me.

We spend the rest of the afternoon catching up on the last

four months, and basking in the beautiful summer day. A part of me starts sewing itself back together; the part that needed Asher so much but couldn't heal without him.

S ummer in London is like nowhere else. We're a people consumed by rain and fog, but for two short months, the weather is brilliant and the city is gleeful.

It's a paradise, meant for school children to play until dark and teenagers to roam the warm air after midnight, up to no good.

"But we're not normal teenagers," I whisper as my fingers lace through Nora's hand.

"Stop being such a baby, don't you go out after midnight all the time?" Her red hair blows in the moonlight, and I can't help but watch this angelic creature lead me along the beach.

At my suggestion, we took the train down to Brighton Beach for the weekend. We booked a room at a little bed-and-break-fast, and spent the last two days traipsing around the beach town, spending time on the rocky beaches and playing carnival games at the boardwalk. It's been the perfect getaway, just time for her and I to bask in the last days of summer.

We've spent the better part of a month and a half wrapped up in each other. When she's not with her family or Eloise, and I'm not rowing or having Ed and Drake over at the flat, we are

together. We don't talk about how she's going to leave at the end
of the warm days, we don't talk about what we are or if we'll
continue this. There is a freedom that comes with not defining
it, but there is also a pressure in my chest every time I think
about her flying halfway across the world and never looking
back.

"Why do we have to come out here now? We already saw the
beach in the daylight," I argue with her, freaked out about being
out here alone.

To be honest, I am being a giant wanker. Usually if I'm out
this late, it's in a limo or at a nightclub. Out here, with nothing
but the waves and the silence and this beautiful girl, I'm a little
shaken.

"Because this is romantic, and because I want to. And you
have to do whatever I say."

She was right of course ... I'd been spending every minute
with her making up for what I'd done. And although Nora
hadn't said it, I think she was almost there.

We reach the middle of the beach, and she plops down, the
waves the perfect backdrop to the night. "Come on, sit."

I sit down next to her and wrap my arm around her shoulder, rubbing her bare shoulder with my fingertips. I can't wait to
get her back to the hotel room, to undress her like I've done for
so many nights now. To worship her exactly how she deserves.

"Isn't it beautiful? When I grow up, I'm moving somewhere
that I can look at the ocean every single day. It's always fascinated me." Her voice is breathless.

I press a kiss into her cheek. "Maybe you should study
oceans then."

She turns her head and tilts it, curiosity peaking her expression. "Maybe I should."

Nora leans her body into mine and rests her head on my
shoulder. "Sometimes I just want to sit here at the ocean's edge

and think about how small and insignificant we are. Like none of this royal, celebrity drama matters at all. None of the money or privilege matters."

Her words stir something inside of me, and I look out into the water, trying to find the meaning she's looking at.

"Maybe we are. Maybe none of it matters. But I like to think that there is a reason we were brought into that same world. The one of spoils and extras. I was blind before I met you, Nora. Stumbling around in the excess and ridiculousness. You showed me, after me fighting you tooth and nail, that there are more important things than money and power. Connections, people, love … those are the small things that mean so much. They've turned into the big things for me."

Twinkling hazel eyes stare at me in the moonlight. "Like your precious Beatles said, love is all you need."

My heart tingles, the feeling spreading to every crevice of my body. "You know that I love you, right?"

My pulse doesn't speed up, my stomach doesn't drop. I'm so sure of my words, so normal with how they feel rolling out of my mouth. This is how I feel about her, and before she goes, she needs to know it.

"Well, now I do." Her lips press together and she tilts her chin, capturing my own mouth.

Under the moonlight we kiss, the crash of the water drowning out the small sighs Nora emits. She doesn't say it back to me, she doesn't need to. Right now, in this moment, there are no promises and no plans being made. And I am completely okay with that.

The glorious summer sun sets over the buildings, the rays casting shadows in every part of the apartment.

"I'm kind of going to miss this place."

"You could stay, you know."

It's the first time he's mentioned me staying, but it's not like he's asking. Asher hasn't begged me to stay, and I haven't offered it. There was an unspoken agreement this summer not to speak about the future. About what came next.

"Don't get all sappy on me now, Frederick." I saunter over to where he sits on the couch, the TV playing some soccer game on the opposite wall.

"Do you want anymore of this before I put it away?" He points to the Indian food sprawled out on the coffee table.

It's our weekly Friday night takeout date, and I'm sad it will be our last. I leave for Pennsylvania tomorrow, and I push the thoughts out of my head, trying not to let them cloud our last night together. The past two months have been wonderful, and my heart squeezes at the thought of not seeing Asher every day.

But I know I have to go.

"No, I'm full. It was delicious, per usual. I brought a little something special." I walk to my bag and pull out the bottle I've been keeping in there.

"And here I thought you don't drink, love." He smiles that crooked, cocky smile.

"Well, I thought that it was a little celebration." I set the bottle of champagne down on the table. "Plus, you know that I do like a little bubbly every now and then."

It's amazing what a couple of months can do. When I first met him, he'd been power-hungry and into the scene, going out and causing havoc. Now? Most nights Asher and I just hang out at his apartment, go out to dinner, or go to the theater. We never party anymore, acting more like a middle aged couple than the freshly minted nineteen-year-olds we are. But I guess that's what crisis and growing up was all about. Asher hadn't been acting his age for years, too old for an innocent life. And I ... I was thrust into growing up. With the press and what happened with Mom and Bennett ... I had never been irresponsible, but the past year had really made me start seeing things in a new light.

Asher pops the top and pours us each some champagne in two coffee mugs. He may have a trust fund and an apartment in Chelsea, but he sure is the eternal bachelor. Plates and a comforter from Primark and coffee mugs are his only source of housewares. It's charming and so normal, it still makes me smile.

"That is some good champagne. You must be rich." Asher grins over the lip of his mug.

I snuggle into him, relishing the feel of his arms. "I'm not, but I know someone with great taste."

We sip our champagne, holding on to each other like we're scared the clock will hit midnight and one of us will turn into a pumpkin.

After a while, the bubbles invade my brain, bliss spreading over my bones. I don't want to talk anymore, and Asher can sense it. He takes the glass from my hand, and sets it down on the table next to his.

Gently, he holds his hand out to me and I take it, and together we walk to his bedroom. The simple queen bed sits against the wall, unassuming. A sadness sweeps over me that it may be the last time I sleep next to him, but I push it aside.

We meet in the middle, our lips seeking each other, trying to express everything we can't say in this moment. Our bodies melt together, doing the things we've learned how to do expertly.

Each touch, each taste, awakens the part of me that only Asher knows how to speak to. My core ignites when he pulls the straps of my romper down, pushing the material past my hips until it pools at my feet. Once his hands start to explore, I can't help but ache for the touch of his skin against my own fingers. His shirt is there and gone in a second, both of us helping to take it off.

Once we're skin-to-skin, it's as if the gun has gone off and no one is waiting for the sprint to the finish. We may be going slow, but nibbles and sucks and strokes are everywhere. Each piece of my flesh lights up as he plays it like a finely tuned instrument. And in turn I key him up, cataloging every noise and reaction, storing it away for a rainy day.

The covers are pulled back and hot skin meets cool sheets. The creak of the bedside drawer has my core blushing, knowing what's coming. And then he's over me, his eyes holding the things we don't say. All of the love between us gets trapped between the blankets, swirling around and igniting our bones as he slowly slides into me.

Our gasps mix in the air, colliding as our hips meet and retreat, meet and retreat. This isn't sex, this isn't craving another body. Tonight is charged with emotion. Asher rocks into me slowly, our hands never parting and our eyes never breaking.

When we finally reach the edge, a tear rolls down my cheek.

Something is slipping right through my fingers, and I can't grab hold.

So I pull Asher as close as I can, memorizing his scent, his feel, his face in the moment that he unravels. A new chapter is beginning, one where I'll have to leave him behind. And while the future is bright, it is also bitter.

I let myself fall asleep in his arms, reveling in the last moments of summer and Asher.

EPILOGUE
NORA

Six Months Later

I wrap the coat a little tighter around my neck, the cold city wind whipping at the wool. Unmelted patches of snow line the streets, dotting the sidewalks like puffs of dirty clouds.

All around me, people bustle to their destination, seeking warmth. My books jostle in the shoulder bag I have slung over my right arm, and as I near the building, I can't wait to get inside. The blast of hot air greets me like a warm friend, and I shake away the cold sticking to my bones.

It's where I come most every day. To stem the anxiety, to get my brain off of being alone in a city that feels like home but also like the strangest place on earth. The gym has become my haven, something I never thought I'd say. But running the miles, lifting the heavy objects ... it seems to calm my panic attacks in a way that I've never been able to conquer them before.

With the extra studying and course load of my first semester of freshman year, I've tried to keep myself as even keel as possible. Coming out of the fall with straight As and a plan on what I wanted to do—oceanography and marine geology—I felt grounded and on track.

But I still felt lonely. I'd made friends, some nice girls on my floor helped to pull me out of my funk and show me some great places around Philadelphia. Bennett and Mom made a monthly trip out, which I told them was unnecessary, but they insisted that it was good for international relations.

And I missed Asher. A lot. I hadn't found, or tried even, to branch out and date since coming to UPenn. There were a couple of guys I'd encountered who seemed like they would have liked to ask, but I shut it down before they were even able to. We texted now and then, talked on the phone when either of us got a free half an hour with the time difference and all of our activities. Which was close to never. All in all, I hadn't heard much from him.

I think we both realized how hard it was, keeping in touch but wondering if the other was seeing someone. Wondering what was happening when either of us wasn't there. We were leading separate lives, and though I missed him like a gaping hole in my heart, I couldn't bring myself to emotionally hurt anymore. And that's what would happen if we talked every day. Because just talking wouldn't be enough.

"Hey, Nora." One of the girls at the front desk waves to me as I walk in.

The campus might be big, but I'm here at the same time everyday, so the staff has come to know me. "Hey, Beth. Cold out there today."

She nods. "Frigid. But hopefully next month brings us some better weather."

I hold up my crossed fingers at her and head downstairs to the locker room. Throwing my book bag, jacket and hat in the locker, I tie my hair up in a ponytail and make my way to the section of the fitness center that houses all of the treadmills and elliptical machines. Popping my headphones into my ears, I hit play on my selection of gym-approved music and get to work.

My legs pound the tread, adrenaline warming my muscles up. In front of the floor-to-ceiling windows, I watch my reflection sprint as the cold wind blows up drifts of snow from the sidewalk. Sweat drips down my back, and my music bumps to the beat in my head. Slowly, I feel the tension drain from my body, nothing left but the focus on breathing and making it through the next mile.

When I finally finish, four miles in thirty-five minutes, I'm tired and sated. Typically, I'd do twenty or thirty minutes of weight work, but for some reason I don't want to. Deciding to listen to my body, I walk the stairs down to the locker room.

Only to run smack dab into a tall body when I round the corner.

"Oof, I'm sorry." A familiar British accent hits my ears, and my entire body relaxes and goes stiff at the same time.

Pulling back, I blink so hard that I feel like my eyeballs might fall out. "What in the world are you doing here? Is this real?"

I reach out, touching the body I've touched so many times, but not in a very long time.

A chuckle rings out as I brush my hand down his T-shirt covered abs. "If this was a dream, would you be able to touch me?"

"I don't know, I'm not sure how that all works. Asher! What are you doing here?" I feel close to tears.

He takes my hand and pulls me around the corner, where we can have a little more privacy from the prying eyes that have begun to watch us. I feel delirious, out of my body. Things like this don't happen to me. But I guess ... I am my mother's daughter and she was whisked off of her feet by a prince so maybe they do.

"Well, I'm getting in my first workout with the rowing team." His green eyes take multiple sweeps of my body, seeming to inventory if everything is still the same.

I hit his shoulder. "Wiseass, not here, in this fitness center ... what are you doing here, in Pennsylvania?!"

I'm still in such shock that I can't keep my voice down. I want to both talk to him and tackle him at the same time.

His brow arches, and he gives a cheeky grin. "Oh, you mean that. So ... I went to Oxford first term, as you know, and when it was time to go back, I just couldn't. I'm not cut out for the prestige and pompous attitudes anymore. Every person there measured me up to the Frederick name, and I got tired of it. I needed a change, a new tradition. And I miss you, bloody miss you like crazy. So I put in my transfer papers and decided to take my first prolonged trip to the States."

My system is freaking out, every inch of excitement and built-up feeling of needing him bursting out at once. I don't hesitate anymore, but jump into his arms, Asher's strong muscles catching me up as I crush my mouth to his.

Tidal waves of this feeling, the sense of coming home, crash into me. With each meeting of our lips, the rhythm of our tongues moving together, overwhelming relief floods me.

"I've missed you so much." I press my head into his shoulder, breathing him in.

He strokes my ponytail. "I couldn't bear to be away for one more bloody minute. Where you are, I need to be."

I raise my head, my body sliding down his as he lowers me to the ground. Our eyes connect and I'm mesmerized.

"I love you, too. I'm sorry I didn't say it before I left, but I felt it."

Asher looks up to the ceiling, letting out a breath. "You don't know what it means to hear you say that."

His hands cup my cheeks, rubbing my skin and looking

straight into my eyes. When our lips connect again, it's as if we both haven't taken a breath in quiet some time.

It's not a fairy tale, so far from it with my sweaty gym clothes and our franticness to be alone in a building with hundreds of students. But I wouldn't have it any other way.

When Asher had said that I'd taught him there were more important things than power and money, I knew he'd taught me too. Before I met him, I didn't have a clue what love was. Not passionate, all-consuming, companionable, can't-live-without-it love. He'd taught me many things about myself, but how to truly love, through flaw and fear, was the most important lesson of all that we'd learned together.

And as we walked hand and hand into the brisk winter night, I looked at the place that used to be my home. The one that just hours ago, felt so strange and lonely. London had felt like that too.

But with Asher by my side, that emptiness no longer existed. Being invisible, floating through life, hadn't made me happy ... and neither had money or status. He was the thing that made it all worth it. And now, we had a completely fresh start to do just that.

Be happy.

Do you want your **FREE** Carrie Aarons eBook?

All you have to do is **sign up for my newsletter**, and you'll immediately receive your free book!

ALSO BY CARRIE AARONS

Read Eloise's story, Elite, now!

Standalones:

Love at First Fight

Nerdy Little Secret

That's the Way I Loved You

Fool Me Twice

Hometown Heartless

The Tenth Girl

You're the One I Don't Want

Privileged

Elite

Red Card

Down We'll Come, Baby

As Long As You Hate Me

All the Frogs in Manhattan

Save the Date

Melt

When Stars Burn Out

Ghost in His Eyes

On Thin Ice

Kissed by Reality

The Callahan Family Series:

Warning Track

The Rogue Academy Series:

The Second Coming

The Lion Heart

The Mighty Anchor

The Nash Brothers Series:

Fleeting

Forgiven

Flutter

Falter

The Flipped Series:

Blind Landing

Grasping Air

The Captive Heart Duet:

Lost

Found

The Over the Fence Series:

Pitching to Win

Hitting to Win

Catching to Win

Box Sets:

The Complete Captive Heart Duet

The Over the Fence Box Set

ABOUT THE AUTHOR

Author of romance novels such as The Tenth Girl and Privileged, Carrie Aarons writes books that are just as swoon-worthy as they are sarcastic. A former journalist, she prefers the love stories of her imagination, and the athleisure dress code, much better.

When she isn't writing, Carrie is busy binging reality TV, having a love/hate relationship with cardio, and trying not to burn dinner. She's a Jersey girl living in Texas with her husband, daughter, son and Great Dane/Lab rescue.

Please join her readers group, Carrie's Charmers, to get the latest on new books, as well as talk about reality TV, wine and home decor.

You can also find Carrie at these places:
Website
Facebook
Instagram
Twitter
Amazon
Goodreads